Charles Armstrong Fox

Lyrics From the Hills

Charles Armstrong Fox

Lyrics From the Hills

ISBN/EAN: 9783744787536

Printed in Europe, USA, Canada, Australia, Japan

Cover: Foto ©Andreas Hilbeck / pixelio.de

More available books at **www.hansebooks.com**

LYRICS FROM THE HILLS.

LYRICS FROM THE HILLS

BY

CHARLES ARMSTRONG FOX.

LONDON:
ELLIOT STOCK, 62, PATERNOSTER ROW, E.C
1891.

Dedication.

TO MY ONLY SISTER.

No beauty e'er flashed on me, but 'twas wed
   With instant vow to share it straight with thee—
The wildest vision from the mountain head,
   When dying day thrust in my hand the key
Of other worlds—the foaming torrent's bed—
   Quaint bridge or gable, heath, or fir-crowned lea
Ah, mighty mother-heart, since thou art fled,
   Mad avarice of eye !—what boots it me ?

Forsaken now that rock-seat in the glen
   We built with glee for thee to rest upon
Beside the murmuring moorland waters, when
   Blue heavens came down to cool themselves
     noon,
And Autumn's gorgeous palette tossed away,
Thy pencil dared the magic waste to stay !

PREFATORY NOTE.

God has written two books, the Book of Nature and the Book of Grace. Both are divine, both are written to be read, both demand study. Each throws light on the other. The Book of Nature is the book of plates to which the written Word is the text. The Book of Plates was published first, for children must first be taught by picture—the text followed long after. Christ found the world teeming with dormant parables. To Him parables from Nature were inevitable. Moral and eternal truth met Him everywhere as He passed along the highways of Time. ' Thy Name how near, Thy wondrous works declare.'

I dare to say these divine analogies and symbolic voices all around us demand more attention than they usually receive, and are pregnant with much meaning hitherto but little recognised. Messages from the Eternal are audible everywhere, if we would but stop and listen. He who runs may read, he who stops may hear. Country holidays thereby become holy days, full of wayside sacraments, and festive spirit tidings, glad surprises of beauty and love from the infinite Father. Poetry is, perhaps, the best vehicle for these communications, because poetry is the most sensitive of all spoken languages, conveying the most delicate shades of meaning which prose often suffers to escape. It is the most refined and delicate of all dialects, and yet it is the noblest, mightiest, and manliest of all. It is the chosen channel of all spiritual, moral, and natural beauty and energy. Poetry is speech with the bloom upon it, it is thought all alive and in flower, it is life ennobled and inspired.

I believe Nature is intended to be an important factor in our education spiritually, as well as mentally and physically. The imaginative faculty is an additional sense, instead of being a want of sense, as many suppose. It discovers the touch of God everywhere; in the rudest elements of human life, as in the loftiest researches of latest science, or the loneliest recesses of Nature. The poetic instinct is the faculty of seeing beauty and of saying the beautiful, and of vitalizing all it sees and says.

'The invisible things of Him from the creation of the world are clearly seen, being understood by the things that are made.'

CONTENTS.

x Contents.

Contents.

YORKSHIRE MOORS.

SURREY HILLS.

DEVONSHIRE HILLS.

WELSH HILLS.

LUDGATE HILL TO RICHMOND HILL.

SYRIAN HILLS—SACRED SONNETS.

SYRIAN HILLS—FOUR TYPICAL WRESTLERS IN HOLY WRIT.

SONNETS AND OTHER PIECES IN MEMORIAM.

' There are, it may be, so many kinds of voices in the world
and none of them is without signification.'

PRAYER BEFORE NATURE.

ANOINT mine eyes with eye-salve, mighty Saviour,
  As through this wonder-world of Thine I stray ;
Let nought in my soul's gesture or behaviour
  Obstruct sweet glimpses of Thyself to-day.

Lift this poor earth-born being to Thy stature,
  Unfold to my rapt spirit one by one
The mighty symbols of mysterious Nature,
  Made luminous with more than mortal sun.

Quicken within me springs of inspiration,
  Visions of beauty bless as they appear,
Leave the fair dream round each new revelation,
  Keep Thou the bloom of distance on the near.

I

Teach me to catch 'twixt lights and shadows fleeing,
 From blossoming dust to rudest crest uphurled,
The murmur and the melody of being,—
 The hymn, in parts, that's chanted round the
  world.

Interpret to love's innocent child-wonder—
 Wonder which knowledge deepens, not dispels—
Decked with fair colours both above and under,
 This home where Time's mysterious childhood
  dwells.

Humanity's sweet tasks by day unfolden
 Let not star-mysteries obscure from sight ;
Nor fierce suns quench with proud ambitions golden
 The moon's white dream of holiness last night.

O'er dancing eyes of wild imagination,
 Quaffing tumultuous rapture ever new,
Lay Thine o'ershadowing Hand in consecration,
 Till sacraments of beauty rise to view.

Surprised in the fine meshes of Thy Being,
 If my tense soul feel round her with strange awe,
Let tears soon wash the avenues of seeing,
 And love find rest by leaning upon law.

Earth is but Heaven's apparel—let each gesture
    Betray the immortal spirit struggling through—
As oft through flying folds of noon's bright vesture
    Break glorious rents of speechless sapphire blue.

If the wild sunbeam flying should allure me,
    Like skirts of immortality revealed,—
If far peaks kindling into speech ensure me
    Secrets of Heaven from Nature's lips unsealed—

Whether the golden Summer open-hearted
    Fling her blue mantle o'er the hills at noon :
Or breezy Autumn's sheaf of beams disparted
    Smite fondly the brown fells all russet-strewn—

Let me in nothing miss Thy Spirit meaning,
    But carried deep into the heart of things,
Veil after veil rent, nought now intervening,
    I'll pierce the shrine of Nature's inmost springs.

Bowed on the riven granite, I adore Thee,
    Earthquake and fire already have been here—
Pass, in procession pass, Great God, before me,
    My soul stands forth uncovered, wrapt in fear—

Anoint mine eyes with eye-salve for the seeing,
    Then to my awestruck soul Thyself announce
Love's Names—dread reservoirs of all life's being,
    Like heaven's high stars bent o'er all lands at once.

Missing Page

Missing Page

Life's disappointments are veiled Love's appoint
 ment—
 Angels of rescue travelling in disguise !
Thanksgiving is the odour of the ointment
 That fills the house of meanest sacrifice.

Then glory to Thee for visions that lie wasted,
 For shrines of haunting beauty still untrod,
For revelations shed abroad untasted !
 And glory to the glorious Will of God !

If shrouding mists should force day to surrender
 His crowning rapture—sunset's golden sea—
Pour Thou Thine own unutterable splendour,
 Thou wounded Face that light'st eternity !

A SUMMER BENEDICITE.

THE DEPARTURE.

Worn out with wars on Nature's laws,
Loud sinning City at our doors
Adieu ! I seek new vital stores,
　　　Where thymy turf
　　　And singing surf
Shall gently heal my spirit sores.

Now welcome din and dusty way,
And welcome too each dull delay
That holds my clamouring hopes at bay,
　　　And swells the glee
　　　No eye can see—
Youth's tumult that no looks betray !

THE ARRIVAL AND FIRST SURVEY.

YE hills whose blue waves bound my sight,
And breeze-swept lakes that beamy bright
Run ribbed with racing lines of light,—
        The antient mirth
        Of sinless Earth
Brings back to man his wasted might,—
            My soul, sing Benedicite.

Ye glorious cataracts that leap
In dazzling light from steep to steep,
While feasts of brokenness ye keep
        All bridal white—
        Sing day and night—
" Rent souls alone soul-whiteness reap,"
            Ye too sing Benedicite.

Ye valleys hidden in the hills,
Each with its flock of bright green fields,
That fragrance, food, contentment yields,
        While homesteads share
        With hill-sides bare
The lonely music of the rills !
            Ye too sing Benedicite.

Ye flying rain-storms that alight
And spread the vales with rainbows bright,
Broad, vivid, low, from height to height,
  And in the lake
  What colours wake,
Till darkness blossoms with delight !
    Ye too sing Benedicite.

Ye thousand torrents at a birth
Fled racing down from heaven to earth
With tidings, tidings,—Life's gone forth !
  White sinless feet
  Down careworn street
And desperate chasm flash new mirth !
    Ye too sing Benedicite.

Ye leafy sanctuaries that hide
In glens beneath the lone hill-side,
Where worship drawn from far and wide
  Holds all the air
  Long hushed in prayer,
And sabbaths all week long abide !
    Ye too sing Benedicite.

Ye mountain-tops, that mute afar
No comrade know save cloud or star,
Yet shed down through Life's stormy war,
    From steep to steep
    Profound and deep
The hills' eternal leisure far !
        Ye too sing Benedicite.

Ye high rock-gashes in the hills,
Where white with foam-flowers, bursting rills,
All silver leaps and liquid thrills,
    Down chiming stairs
    In crystal pairs
Now leap, now loiter, on rock-sills !
        Ye too sing Benedicite.

Ye mountain streams that long unheard
On mighty uplands slept unstirred,
Now plunging past like shyest bird,
    Or shy souls known
    Alas, when flown,
Or poets buried to be heard !
        Ye too sing Benedicite.

Ye beauty-haunted souls, whose feet
From crag to crag while pulses beat
Still breathless chase bright blooms that fleet,
      Pause grateful now
      On this high brow—
Where currents of God's mercies meet !
         Ye too sing Benedicite.

Ye poet souls that steal along,
Unheard, unguessed, your gurgling song,
Who feel round Nature's heart, nor wrong
      Her inspired mood
      With raptures rude,
Struck dumb by revelations strong !
         Ye too sing Benedicite.

Ye breezes off the hills of God,
Like wings inhaled I spurn the clod,
And, drunk with breath of mountain sod,
      I buoyant bathe
      My limbs, and swathe
In waves of fountain coolness proud !
         Ye too sing Benedicite.

Ye copses, where Spring loves to greet
With mist of bluebells early feet,
And (spiritual vision sweet !)
      Mid darkest bowers
      Large milk-white showers
Of cherry blooms we start to meet !
         Ye too sing Benedicite.

Ye wild woods now like sobered age,
When eager childhood's brimming page,
And pictured dreams, no more engage
      Enraptured souls,—
      But through dark boles
Gold sunset rifts life's cares assuage !
         Ye too sing Benedicite.

Ye huge twin peaks, stupendous peers
Of this wild realm, gray deathless seers
That scan unmoved the trackless years !
      Let silence keep
      Her awful sleep,
Avenge with peace earth's shattered ears !
         Ye too sing Benedicite.

Ye wild crags wet with thunder rains,
And scourged with storms, till bursting veins
Of flashing silver chase your stains,
      And sunlit mist,
      Gold, amethyst,
Spreads glory's court mid steaming plains !
           Ye too sing Benedicite.

Ye glittering seas, where clad in white,
Through open windows of the night,
The virgin Moon walks forth as bright
      As that first day
      She shone away
Death's shadow, Sleep, with deathless light !
           Ye too sing Benedicite.

A SUMMER DAY AMONG THE HILLS.

Ye quickening skies and growing light,
And sleeping vales all misty white,
And couching kine's moist dew-forms bright,
      And air from heaven
      Divinely given
To bathe the temples of the night !
           Ye too sing Benedicite.

Ye summer dawns, white dawns all dew,
Where sun-smit peaks break travelling through,
And startled meres gleam back to view,
  And shadows dip
  O'er brimming lip
For their first baptism of blue !
    Ye too sing Benedicite.

Ye days of heaven, when past all art
Wild Nature brimming every part
Breaks open her great summer heart
  In one wide feast
  To man and beast,
And shadowy guests strange lore impart !
    Ye too sing Benedicite.

Ye haunts of bliss, where Heaven and we,
Together ranging hill and lea,
Spent days in golden company,
  And Nature spread
  Like daily bread
Her sacrament of colours free !
    Ye too sing Benedicite.

Ye glowing symbols, visions grand
Of that mysterious summer land
Of Immortality, whose strand
      All golden fair
      Floats hid in air,
And any moment we may land !
           Ye too sing Benedicite.

Ye blooms, soft blooms, bright, empyreal !
Whose blue breath, like God's first ideal
Still clinging, floating, round the real,
      Veils Nature's face
      In spirit grace
And depths of dreamlight hymeneal !
           Ye too sing Benedicite.

Ye ancient forest glades and halls
Green, grassy, silent ; aisles and walls
Lone echoing to the thrush's calls—
      Aisles dim and old
      With sunny gold
Fresh paved for Summer festivals !
           Ye too sing Benedicite.

Ye startled creatures of the wood,
Fur faces that with timorous brood
Dart back !—we're all one brotherhood—
    Own one great Lord,
    Sit at one board,
Guests too dependent to be rude !
        Ye too sing Benedicite.

Ye sovereign heights and glory-lands,
Where sun and shadow linking hands,
In soundless song, far-ranging bands,
    Stir all the hills
    With joy that stills
And adoration that expands !
        Ye too sing Benedicite.

Ye wild brooks, leapt from skyey lairs,
Dance down your grand old mountain stairs
To music of primeval airs !—
    Through thunder bowers
    Burst, crystal flowers—
Wild blossoms of a thousand years !
        Ye too sing Benedicite.

Ye wastes and silences that wait
Round gray creation's outer gate,
Half 'twixt create and uncreate,
        Noon's splendours haste
        To clothe the waste,
Eve's camping glories linger late !
                Ye too sing Benedicite.

Ye fastnesses and mountains drear,
No voice save falling torrent near,
No wealth of pictured hues ye wear,
        A few slow scars
        From Time's long wars
Are all the hoarded wealth ye bear !
                Ye too sing Benedicite.

Ye tarns secreted in the fold
Of mighty hills hoar ages old,
Whose sealèd lips may ne'er unfold
        What lidless eyes
        Without surprise
Through sleepless centuries behold !
                Ye too sing Benedicite.

Ye rock-peaks scorning earth's flushed fells,
None change their raiment here, nought tells
The flight of Time !—in fitful swells
　　　Far torrents chime
　　　From towers sublime
Through countless aisles their ghostly bells !
　　　　　　Ye too sing Benedicite.

Ye slanting beams whose radiance fills
The mighty bosom of the hills
With mystic fervours, and distils
　　　O'er yonder plain
　　　A glorious rain,
Where crowding splendour broods and stills !
　　　　　　Ye too sing Benedicite.

Ye worlds of shadows wandering wide
In mighty flocks, without a guide,
Now shouldering up the huge hill's side
　　　In phantom haste—
　　　Now joined by vast
Impersonal glooms born as light died !
　　　　　　Ye too sing Benedicite.

Ye sunsets and flushed headlands bold,
While altar flames grow grandly cold,
What vistas of far worlds unfold—
> What flashing prints
> And glory-hints
Of footsteps of no mortal mould !
> > Ye too sing Benedicite.

Ye fading woodlands, glimmering stream,
And blackbird's last wild juicy scream,
Night-beetle's vagrant hum !—I deem
> Stillness can teach
> Divinest speech,
Silence with loftiest converse teem !
> > Ye too sing Benedicite.

Ye moon-lit meres mid mountains hoar,
Where at each dip of muffled oar
Smooth silver wrinkles chase your floor,
> And liquid bliss
> Doth lie and kiss
With dreamy lips the enchanted shore !
> > Ye too sing Benedicite.

Ye silver nights, when bridal bright
Earth's spiritual guests alight
Mid listening leaves the livelong night,
  And all the air
  Divinely fair
Is whitened with celestial light !
    Ye too sing Benedicite.

Ye prophet souls that may not stay
Imprisoned in this narrow clay,
But rapt in visions far away
  Mid burning hymn
  Of seraphim
With the long night enlarge the day !
    Ye too sing Benedicite.

Ye thought-blocks loosed from quarried brain,
Slow floating down the solemn main
Of meditation, noiseless train !
  Though late ye reach
  The ports of speech
And Fame's proud temple steps ye gain !
    Ye too sing Benedicite.

AN AUTUMN DAY AMONG THE HILLS.

YE midnight Heavens serene and strong,
Star-pierced eternities, where Wrong
Still casts cloud-stains, but not for long—
    For Heaven's high rest
    Mysterious, blest,
Woos suffering earth to join her song!
       Ye too sing Benedicite.

Ye fire-crowned hills, height kindling height,
All spell-bound watching out of sight
The mighty moveless march of Light,
    Whose soaring head
    As from the dead
Through blossoming heavens burns forth in might!
       Ye too sing Benedicite.

Ye wild birds fresh from holt and hurst
Vociferous, in volleys burst
On raids of happy hunger, first
    Saluting day
    With deafening play—
Love-quarrels through night-slumbers nurst!
       Ye too sing Benedicite.

Ye hamlet Towers, whose sheltering wings
Guard each its brood of cots that clings
And nestles round life's sabbath springs,
    Where hope divine,
    And Heaven's glad wine
Flows free, and want drinks deep and sings !
        Ye too sing Benedicite.

Ye mountain lawns, and autumn days,
And breezy, bracken-scented ways,
And far peaks fondled by fair rays,
    Who, who can tell
    Your mighty spell—
The bliss, the pain of speechless praise !
        Ye too sing Benedicite.

Ye autumn steeps few eyes discern,
All purple glooms and gleams by turn,
Where orange swarth of sun-scorched fern
    Like glorious rust
    Thick with gold dust
Makes all the hill-sides glow and burn !
        Ye too sing Benedicite.

Ye boundless moorlands rolling free,
Bare pools, rocks, verdure, one wild sea,
Where Time mates with Eternity,
  And health and heather
  Range on together
Down perfumed paths of liberty !
    Ye too sing Benedicite.

Ye huge wastes, like fair worlds begun
Left shapeless, where rich blooms, blue, dun,
And gorgeous colours melt and run,
  And wild birds breed,
  And ripe gorse seed
Now snaps its fingers in the sun !
    Ye too sing Benedicite.

Ye cloud-rifts, and wild sheaf of beams
Shot headlong, till the mountain teems
With arrowy splendours ! your pale streams,
  Though high noon now,
  Yon mountain's brow
Have blanched as with white light of dreams !
    Ye too sing Benedicite.

Ye beamy ladders that alight,
Where misty pilgrimages bright
In slow procession throng the height,
    While halos float
    Where sunbeams smote,
And brim far vales with dust of light !
        Ye too sing Benedicite.

Ye leagues of golden woods, and spires
Of black blue pines, red maple fires,
Grand conflagration of the shires—
    The dying year
    From her gold bier
Sighs farewell through wrecked woodland choirs !
        Ye too sing Benedicite.

Ye solemn brotherhood of peaks,
Jostling each other yet none speaks,
Stern sabbath of eternal weeks,
    Where all who come
    Pass out hence dumb,
None gives, nor information seeks !
        Ye too sing Benedicite.

Ye mountain glooms that trend away,
And cliffs inexorably gray,
Where one tall single lance-like ray
      Leans high alone
      By desert throne,
Like staff of angel gone astray !
           Ye too sing Benedicite.

Ye rainbows flushing hill and wood,
Heaven's phantom storm-flower gracious, good,
That flying blossoms where wrath stood !
      Though storm ne'er knew
      Whose retinue
Concealed the angel of the Flood !
           Ye too sing Benedicite.

Ye flying gleams, wild lights of God,
Through rents in some unseen abode
Of blessedness escaped abroad,
      Whose magic glance
      As if by chance
Doth spiritualize the meanest sod !
           Ye too sing Benedicite.

Ye bounding breezes, wrestling woods,
And sheen of flying showers, and floods,
Bright floods in singing multitudes,
  And at my feet
  In this retreat
White daisies' pouting purple buds !
     Ye too sing Benedicite.

Ye western crags, huge herded flocks,
That, pent in yon blue fold of rocks,
Couch dreamlike draped with gorgeous shocks
  Of sunset mist
  All glory-kissed,
And leonine huge purple locks !
     Ye too sing Benedicite.

Ye hills and vales, and lakes retired,
And sunset earth all glory fired,
I gaze, and gaze, till half inspired,
  And yet I thirst
  For Him who first
Dug wells of beauty undesired !
     Ye too sing Benedicite.

(Dumb Nature beckons me away,
From height to height, from day to day,
Thence some new feature to display
    Of her great Lord,—
    Some sunlit hoard—
" Come, bless me Him from hence, I pray,
    Oh, join earth's Benedicite !")

Ye altars of the lowland sod,
Ye mountain shrines man's feet ne'er trod,
Ye soaring heavens, past Time's abode,
    O'er Time and ties—
    I rise, I rise,
To thee, free, boundless, ever-nearing God !
    I too sing Benedicite.

Great God, enthroned in light sublime,
Still lingering in the porch of Time
All love-lit, listening the faint climb
    Of human feet—
    Thee, Thee, I greet,
And worship mid earth's sunset chime :
    Crown Thou our Benedicite !

MOUNTAIN WATERBROOKS.

I.

THE PILGRIM'S APPROACH.

I SEE them in the rocks and hills—
The gushing purity that stills
And awes and fascinates the gaze,
Where headlong down their rocky ways,
O'er perilous stairs the waters dash,—
Ah, blessings on yon virgin flash !—
That, bright with innocent amaze,
Breaks foaming through this sullen gash
Deep in the eternal granite's side,
Half hidden by a mountain ash
That waves aloft its crimson pride.

While blackening jaws gape wide asunder,
Still thirsting for the glorious thunder !
So down the ruined stair of Time,
All healing with its mellowing chime,
Mercy, like music, breaks sublime !

II.

THE GATHERING OF THE WATERS ON THE HIGH TABLELANDS.

I HEAR them from the heights afar,
From lonely lands of cloud and star ;
Just launched forth from their crystal home,
With gathering murmurs on they come,—
O'er beds of boulders now rudely tost,
In groves of bracken a moment lost,
Then a liquid flash ! and the echoing host,
Through many a rent and rift of gloom,
Fissure and gully, they come, they come,
Bright bursting, bounding to their doom,—
Over the chasms and over the rocks,
And the black abyss of the thunder blocks,
    From steep to steep,
    As the angels leap,
Like an angel waked from immortal sleep !

Now stripping in glorious throes mid-air
Pale crystal thews and sinews bare,
Till white with rocky war and strife,
Their breathless tidings, life, life, life,
Resound afar !—I hear them all,
The passion and the perilous fall,
The mirth, the music, and the call !

III.

THE SPIRIT OF THE FALL.

Oh ! a wondrous sight,
In the summer light,
Is the stainless soul of the Infinite
Poured forth from its own unapproachable height !
On Love's altar out-poured—
(Love of God, be adored !)
For Love is a priest in her own native right,
In herself sheathed the sword—
(Love of God, be adored !)
And her life-blood is white as unsearchable light ;
And though men turn aside
To adore or deride,

Still alone in her solitude all day and night
    Is that white Soul out-poured !
    (Love of God, be adored !)
    God of Love, matchless Lord !—
    Love of God, be adored !

IV.

THE PILGRIM IN CONTEMPLATION.

Yᴇ broken souls, draw near and gaze,
Heaven here Life's mystery displays !
As through yon glorious granite gate,
The mighty waters, self-compelled,
At one stupendous moment yield
To the high pressure of their fate,—
What inward glory, long concealed,
What beatific vision sealed,
White like God's whiteness, breaks revealed
'Mid earthly weakness, mortal soil !—
Not by slow dint of desperate toil,
But at one plunge of sheer descent,
One bound of bright abandonment,
Brave Love, in eager consecration,
Her brimming sheaves of hope and fear
Pours forth in hungering adoration,—
As yon dread swirl of waters sheer,

Hurled brimming onward where no fence
Protects the chasm (maddening sense !)
Bursts into instant flower of dazzling innocence !—
In crystal raiment bright arrayed
Like the unfallen, yet undismayed !
Such foaming harvest of the rock
Reaped down in one triumphant shock—
Life's instant harvest of long years,
Faith reaps, transfigured in her tears !
O crown of Love, high Self-Surrender,
Whose dazzling, though unconscious, splendour
Robes the whole man in sudden light
Most supernaturally bright—
The majesty of brokenness,
An inward but immortal dress,
The sudden flower of spotlessness !
Thus all anointed souls are crowned
By kneeling first, and being bound
By altar of the Lamb once slain,
In fetters fetterless to reign !
　　Ye wondrous symbols, evermore
Call Faith aside to kneel, adore !
'Mid tumult and the glorious throng,
The shout and everlasting song,
Lo ! altar, smoke, and sacrifice,

Bared ever to the open skies,
And worship, too, that never dies !
White flower of brokenness, fair crown
Of glory, wove of throe and thorn !
What beauty like high sorrow's grace—
The beauty of a brave distress ?
Such moments of high grace faith knows
When souls, o'erborne by sudden woes,
Have unsuspected bridal found—
Just when Faith's last step quit the ground
To darkly plunge into the tomb
With voiceless prayer—Thy kingdom come,
Magnificence of martyrdom !
Dark waters blossom white in breaking,
High souls are made in the unmaking !

V.

THE SPIRIT OF THE FALL.

Ah, Love's broken life-chord,
Love's resounding life-chord,
Who can measure the might of that music outpoured
When by light of Love's wounds shed 'mid dark of the
    fight,
Broken spirits henceforth grown immortal in might

Dare dismay and defeat,
And undo life's retreat !
For this music of death
Is the world's new life-breath—
On, ye soldiers of Life, ever onward !—it saith,
Through stern passes of doubt,
Hark, still onward ! the shout,
Till on heights blue eternity crowned we emerge,—
Still on Heaven's utmost verge,
Past the roar of life's surge,—
Still the music is heard
Of that white Soul outpoured,—
(Lamb of God, be adored !)
As each soul gains the summit exclaiming, "The
Lord !"

VI.

THE PILGRIM IN EXPLORATION.

BROWN moorland mother, brooding wild,
Cradling in awe thy crystal child,
Soon laughing vales thy child shall take
To sing bright songs to them, and make
A mountain mirror of the Lake,—

Whose silent soul with earth inwrought,
Fair living sheet of liquid thought,
Shall think bright thoughts aloud unheard,
While man, still thoughtless as a bird,
Treads these grand by-ways of High God,
The precincts of His own abode,
As if they were the common road,—
Still blind, though throes of Nature here
Have filled the land with glorious fear,
Blind to the healing Hand that hurled
Such beauteous judgments o'er the world !
   Wild nest of living waters, hail !
I've hunted thee from vale to vale,
Climbed one huge chamber in the hill
And then another lonelier still,
Where nought but stag-moss clasps rock-stair,
And moon-green tufts of juniper
Dark stud the waste ; where nought's astir
Save wild bee scolding heather-bells
For lack of honey in their cells.—
Still on I strode ; one more ascent,
And round the rocks, where'er the bent
Of wild will lures thy gleaming feet,
At last I've found thy shy retreat.
Hail, secret seed of moisture ! Spring
Inaudible, thou nameless thing !

Remote on mighty uplands high,
Secreted underneath the sky,
Germs of omnipotence here lie !
Art thou, meek voice invisible,
Thou, the proud source of bursting rill,
And thundering rivulet and broad-backed flood ?
Thy birth-place this lone cloud-kissed hill,
Thy guardians these stern peaks of God ?
Thy mother, the brown moorland wild,
And thou her sky-born mystic child,
Cradled in awe, long dream-beguiled ?
Whence thine omnipotence ? I cried,—
It paused not,—trickling down inside
Its dark bed—I myself replied,—
" Winds fold their wings on ocean's breast,
Strong suns themselves seek rosy rest ;
From dawn till dark thou toilest late,
Last labourer on God's estate,—
From dark to dawn like pauseless fate
Still toiling on, past sunset's flush,
All through long midnight's awful hush,
'Mid darkness and earth's dewy damp,
Still toiling on without a lamp :
'Mid lonely mosses on the height,
And shivering reeds far out of sight,

And mystic murmurs strange and far,
Without the glimmer of a star,
While mortal toil is hushed and still,
Thou still art busy on the hill,—
Still weaving noiselessly a chain
Of waters out of drops of rain,
To fertilize Earth's sleeping plain !"

VII.

THE PILGRIM IN RETROSPECT FROM THE SUMMIT.

AT last from the height of the riven cliff's brow,
I lean o'er the edge of the precipice now !
How cool the moist breath of fierce chasm and cleft
Thunder-riven, save pools of heaven-stillness still left
Dark suspended on perilous ledges far down,
Each with tufts of broad ferns slowly waving, self-sown;
And one frail pensive birch hurled in wrath from its
    place
Still hanging tiptoe o'er the gulf to efface—
Like a breath of forgiveness—the storm's savage trace !
Whence yon gleam through the darkness beneath ?—
    'Tis the Fall
Still breaking afresh with its ceaseless life-call.

Whence this gleam through the dark rent of Time ?—
    'Tis the Lord,
        Who though victor ascended,
        Till time's conflict's ended,
Himself is descended with Spirit-bright sword,
(Like this white-flashing fall with its ceaseless life-
    call !)
        And through darkness of time,
        Self-illumined sublime,
        By the light of His Cross,
        Lest high Heaven suffer loss,
        He still routs the dark host,
        Rallies still the long lost,
        Luring souls through the mist
        By His Cross, glory-kissed,
Which gives back—like this fall—all heaven's light it
    receives,
Whether sun-shafts stream dazzling in arrowy
    sheaves ;—
        Or the moon holds her breath,
        And unheard entereth
This holy of holies, sole-lighted by death !
        And all the night long,
        'Mid the loud thunder song
That isolates most in the heart of the throng,

Through dread veil of white breath
She alone entereth,
Where for ever apart—
In the innermost shrine of that one broken heart,
There shattered all stainless on time's ruined stair,
'Mid ceaseless hosannas ascending and prayer,
Through eternal rocks rent,
There, liked veiled sacrament,
Behold ! Love lays bare to all worshipping eyes
Heaven's costliest, best, and last sovereign surprise,—
In awful whiteness poured God's own stupendous
Sacrifice !

VIII.

THE STILL MOUNTAIN TARN.

High voiceless Tarn like God's eternity,
Deep seated in the summit of the hills,
Whence issue forth perpetual rills
Of virgin light and liberty,—
I feel your silence from afar
Commingling with the world below,
Your secret in my bosom bear
With lightened footsteps as I go ;
Deep in the chamber of my breast
Is lodged your everlasting rest ;

Such rest alone can brave the shocks
And innocent bloodshed of the rocks,
Where torn upon the lacerating steeps,
From ledge to ledge, in passionate leaps,
The wounded waters, as to prove
The quick recovery of Love,
From rock-griefs have new glory wove,—
Thence ceaseless weave all day aloud
A bridal robe instead of shroud,—
Prophetic of that day, rent tomb,
When clad in white from Calvary's dark loom,
The Church's Bridal yet shall burst the gloom !
Then low at bottom of the Fall
By sweet constraint surrendering all,
Deep pools repeat the Tarn on high,
Give back once more the quiet sky,
Like weanèd souls, still, voiceless, lie !

IX.

THE GAIETY OF NATURE'S CHILD-HEART.

Here's a streamlet from the crowd
Talking to herself aloud—
Brimming o'er the ferny edges,
Listening on the rocky ledges,

Plunging down some desperate pass
Angrily, alas, alas !
Flooding noiselessly the mosses,
Boiling round huge boulder bosses,—
Ah, the Frolic, back she tosses
Laughing locks of light !—Then passes
Twinkling in and out the grasses,
Fretting at some broken stair,
Hushed a moment as in prayer ;
Deftly to their island home
Steering dainty fleets of foam ;
Then with every dreamy neighbour
Loitering to complain of labour !—
Gossiping at reedy angle,
Till the inevitable tangle
Of quick words begets a wrangle ;
Reeds and rushes both at once
(Lances bristling !) each denounce :
Wrangling o'er a broken bubble,
Sighing, crying, lots of trouble !
Suddenly face hid away
Darkling ;—sparkling back to day !
What incorrigible play !
Waters, waters, Run away !

X.

THE PILGRIM IN BENEDICTION.

Now blessings on yon darkening skies,
Whence skyborn songs about us rise,
God and the weeping cloud once met
Dark destinies to music set !
For He who brimmed the wild bird's bill
Dark waters tuned to sing His will,
Their liquid voices early taught
To lisp in numbers, till they wrought
Unearthly music, soft and clear—
As if from some invisible choir
Behind the lattice-work of Time
Came voices of a purer clime !
Ye rills, ye wild harps of the hills
Swept by the breeze in sudden thrills,
Wild wandering music of the height
Played loudest to the listening night—-
Ye lonely harps of lonely lands,
Touched softly by invisible hands,
Oft startled by delicious fear,
Man's wandering footsteps pause to hear
Your phantom music on the breeze,
Entangled in bare rocks and trees !

Strange fragments flung from mystic strings,
Like wafts of Inspiration's wings,
Haunt many a dark and secret place
Within the mighty hills' embrace,
Like pilgrim angel's lonely grace—
Enchantments not of Time or Space !

XI.

THE PILGRIM LOST IN REVERIE.

But as I listen like a child,
Drinking the music of the wild—
The bounding of those waters fleet,
The trampling of their mellow feet,
The crystal melody complete—
My heart within me hears a strain,
A still more musical refrain ;
The brightness of the soul's ideal
Seems henceforth blended with the real !
Through human tears and toil of earth
The innocence of God breaks forth,
The holiness of innocent mirth !
A new link binds me to the Throne,
Bright immortality is won,
The dust, the din, of cares is done !

SUNSET ASCENT OF CONISTON OLD MAN.

I.

THE ASCENT.

Our mountain track lay high across the fells—
A road not less inviting to our steps
Because all day long unfrequented now,
Save by wild spring or wandering rivulet,
Sole passengers that murmuring pass that way.
Across the fells, and, bounding many a bed
Of sounding torrent, up the hills we wound
Past Walney Scar, and past the serried edge
Of beetling Dow Crag, whose huge cloven cliff
Loves to entangle in its gloomy horns
The misty rain-cloud—past the shuddering brink,
Where fathoms down in its tremendous chasm

Goatswater sleeps imbedded—on we sped
Spurred by the north wind, and essayed to climb,
Spite the low sun, the mighty western slope
Of Coniston Old Man.—Broad shadows fell
Far reaching downward, peopling with their flocks
Of shifting glooms the mountain's deep defiles.
Rich Autumn lustre from the sinking sun
Lay warm upon the mountain pass ; and far
Seaward, and northward stretching without pause,
Innumerable ridges of huge hills
Stood crowned with misty radiance ; tier on tier,
All couching westward in stupendous rest,
Seemed rapt in worship, as the dying sun,
Like some vast world-atoning sacrifice,
There poured itself away in glorious waste !
But ere we gained the summit's windy height
Or climbed its rock-crest, lo, the broad sun fell,
And left us in a lone and widowed world.
'Twas strange, but at that moment so it chanced,
A raven, startled by our footsteps, rose
Off the bare crag, and croaking o'er us fled,
Leaving us with wild Nature quite alone—
Alone with God's great solemn twilight world.
Deep silence then observed we for a space,
Such silence as 'mid dim cathedral aisles,

When one man's fall has left a whole land mute,
The kneeling multitudes awe-struck maintain,
Breathless, intense—perchance intenser here,
Though without walls this temple—for what shrine
So awful as these lone dread lighted heavens !
Or what high anthem half so thrills the soul
As yon mute flushed peak, now sole worshipper
'Mid all this mighty concourse of wild forms,
Transfixed by yonder fading stair of gold—
Eve's burnt-out sunset's lingering altar stair !
How moving are Earth's antient silences !
Here on this height uplifted 'mid a world,
A solitary world of mountain tops,
How dreadful is this silence !   The far hush
And multitudinous stillness seems to awe
The very air, as if high God had spoken
And suddenly ceased speaking in His might,
Leaving all nature spell-bound !   Yet a voice,
A voice mysterious, unmistakable,
Silence herself unwittingly compels
From these dumb changeless crags, whose riven
      forms,
Although they speak not, ceaselessly give forth
The grand unwritten scriptures of the hills
In Time's primeval language ; and spell out

Here to these naked solitudes aloud,
Slowly in ponderous syllables of awe,
The solemn accents of Eternity
That none may misinterpret.

                    Who from hence,
Standing on this bold headland, who had guessed,
'Mid these wild surging hills whose billows break
Unheard on the horizon, what retreats
By silver waters unsuspected lie !
What leafy sanctuaries lurk 'mid savage rocks,
What sunny secrets golden summer hides
In wildest chasm, loneliest recess,
Leaving them there unguarded all day long
Till sunset !   Ah, what wealth has sunset's ray,
What wealth unshed, till sudden as it smites
The fleeting shower's pale fringes, lo, the beam,
In sweet collision betwixt sun and tears,
Bursts open into blossom like a flower,
Whose glowing petals, gloriously alive,
Leap from their dewy scabbard at a bound,
As Light spreads proudly all her lustrous loom
Unravelling fairest colours !—such Faith's ray,
Faith with no needle but a ray of light
Weaves such immortal tapestries of tears,

All Heaven stoops down to wonder !   Here all day
What glorious revelations shed themselves
Ungazed !   What moving incidents of light,
Of light and shade in Nature's swift romance
For ever shifting, breathless hold the hills,
From morn to eve a whole long summer's day,
Spell-bound as with enchantments !   Loneliest peaks,
Dyed with a thousand sunsets, now seem touched
With almost human pathos ; yea, instinct
(So infinite the play of features there)
Instinct with mystic meaning.   Every cloud
Seems consciously to cast its shadow down,
Like Time's frail wing slow fluttering o'er the brow,
The broad still brow of mute eternity,
Unheard, unheeded !   What new wonders now,
What thrill of supernatural delight,
When rolling mists descending lend to Earth
The spirit-life she longs for !—Crags loom forth,
All wrought about with darkness and life storms,
Loom   fringed   with   hurrying   vapours ;   wreathing
      mists
First heighten, and then hide, then bright betray
Dread secrets of the hills, strange visions veiled
Rent in a radiant moment, rent and read,
Then sealed again, impenetrably sealed

In folds more blinding !   Brightly cleansed away,
What joy to watch, white breasting heaven's blue
        deep,
Some floating cloud with silent shadow climb
And fling its stately mantle o'er the peak,
As some high Presence had alighted there
To hold with earth a moment's fellowship,
Then vanished !
                        Visited alone by clouds,
(And their soft footsteps deepen, not disturb,
The stillness of these mountain solitudes,)
What wild dales echo to the waterbrooks
That veil in foam the passion of their fall ;
What valleys of unbroken sabbath lie
Free as the Heaven above us, and like Heaven
Their fearless gates stand open day and night
For ever, guarded only by the awe
Of native sanctity !   Here careworn hearts
Their long-lost peace recover !   Here from Heaven
Relit in secret, prophet souls descend
To kindle the quenched altars of the world,
Bearing aloft in folded hands of prayer
Safe through this windy world the fire divine !
Here in rapt vision from the mountain's brow
Snatched at this cloudless moment, Faith refired

With all the dread magnificence of Time,
And sunset's crowning splendour of repose,
Yearns once again to pierce the city's roar
And smoke of human battlefields—intent
On spirit spoils, and an immortal goal !
Here by the measure of the sanctuary,
God's sanctuary of the hills, and by her scales,
Dread scales of silence, man remeasures all
Life's petty pastimes ; here recalls how oft
He too, alas, no less than other men,
Has yoked God's priceless team of golden days
To plow long furrows in a bootless soil
For serf's ignoble wages !
                                   But enough—
The silence broken, hastily we rose,
And turning slowly eastward to descend,
Lo ! right against us on the crag unheard,
Stealing upon us from another world,
The huge pale moon stood level with us veiled—
Like some mysterious watcher just emerged
From other heavens to haunt the hills of Time,
Wrapt in her own white loneliness of light.
What wonder if on that seraphic height
Which thus stood forth transfigured over all,
We seemed intruders on that upper world,

Where Sun and Moon, inexorably far
By solemn fate divided, at that hour,
Above that antient solitary peak,
Linking long hands of light across the world,
Had met and gazed, and dying sunset kissed
The faint moon's virgin brow bent towards him
    veiled,
Then parting sped each on its soundless way !
All was unearthly round us, strangely fair,
We seemed new landed on some spirit shore,
Like wanderers who had crossed the bounds of Time
Into some wondrous elemental world,
Where nought e'er interrupts the shining pomp
And slow majestic harmonies of Space !

II.

THE DESCENT.

OUR universal survey at an end,
We quit the summit, slowly now descend
The huge hill's deepening gorges stern and wild,
Shrouded in twilight,—yonder, like a child,
Some lonely mountain child that never smiled—
Born of the very solitude, and high
Slung on the cliff's huge shoulders, we espy

A dark and lonely tarn that shivering lay
Sleepless,—below it but a little way,
And yet cut off from all companionship,
So strict the law of solitude they keep,
Another tarn twin-born hung black as night,
Cradled in crags ;—when round the buttressed height
Quarried and rent, as downward still we urged
Our tired steps, suddenly the path emerged
High on a bare ledge ; there sheer depths beneath,
A thousand fathoms down, where still as death
Black night clung, lo ! a wondrous vision brake—
The full moon walked serenely the far lake
In angel silence ! pleased before her feet,
Rippling in silver scales, dark waters fleet
Noiseless,—the very Christ we seemed to see
Walking again the waves of Galilee !
Again the charmèd waters caught His word,
Straight glistering smoothed their ruffled plumes nor
        stirred,
The God-light falling from His feet unheard !

FURNESS ABBEY.

I LINGERED long 'mid shadows of old time—
The rapt air tingled with some ghostly chime.

Embosomed in low hills and sheltering trees,
Withdrawn in groups like mute assemblages,

Archway and aisle stood bare ;—red mouldering towers
Dark ivy-mailed rose proudly, crowned with showers
Of feathery grasses, weeds, and self-sown flowers

Wherc'er I gazed, soft bowers with their green shade
Through crumbling vistas had an entrance made.

Faint airs went whispering through the ruined halls,
Gray silence sat within the sculptured stalls.

Roofless the fair shrine stood, save Heaven's soft sky
Leaned o'er, and blent its blue eternity !

Each court was paved with verdure rank and deep,
And shattered corbels slept their long green sleep.

Through the high mullioned windows, rent and bare,
Streamed in unhindered the rich summer air—

While from dry joints of antient masonry
Frail ferns slow waved their pensive heraldry.

Nature, now sole surviving worshipper,
Whose noiseless footprint climbed each broken stair,

Drew fondly back into herself again,
Reconsecrated now, that mouldering fane !

No voice of praise was heard, none knelt to pray,
But, from some hoary volume of decay,
The robin read the lesson for the day !

GRASS OF PARNASSUS, NEAR TARN HOWS.

I.

O FAIR, fair Earth, high God built for His children—
    Lit by far worlds, and lined with human love !
Each weed that blows, with innocence bewildering,
    Breaks open some sealed message from above.

I stood and watched the hills' majestic shoulders,
    Broad height o'er height upheaving heather-stained,
While at my feet, 'twixt bog and mountain boulders,
    Large starry milk-white blossoms footing gained—

Grass of Parnassus ! thou shalt be my teacher,
    Lead on, white star, through trackless moorland
        waste,
Thou art the desert's dowry, spotless creature,
    With thy pure ivory petals nobly chaste !

Thine the flushed moorland chasm, with its tangles
  Of sweet bog-myrtle, yew, and feathery ferns—
Thine the wild wreck of tossing crags and angles,
  Sequestered waterfalls, and rude moss-urns.

Gleam out, pale star, from beds of tawny rushes,
  From shades of juniper dark cedar-blue,
From reed-choked channels where wild music gushes—
  True to thine instincts always, nobly true !

II.

Behold, what love God scatters o'er the mountains,
  What tendernesses infinite and rare !
What boundless largess in the laughing fountains,
  That burst forth singing from each rocky lair.

What glorious mountain shoulders never-ending !
  Dark purple ridges first—tumultuous host,
The next gold-fleeced, bright moss and sunshine
        blending,
  Beyond, thick bloom—blue dream—in distance lost.

What daring peaks go soaring up the azure,
  All rent and seamed with grand interstices !
What towering crags, in multitudinous leisure,
  Stretch couching slumbrous in the summer breeze

What breezes dwell upon each trackless summit,
  Life-giving, pure, like life-breath from the Throne!
What depths unfathomed by all human plummet,
  Where God Almighty's sun-rays walk alone!

What stately rays strike deep to earth's foundation,
  Like angel compasses o'er mortals bent!
What bursting beams outstretched in grand vibration,
  Like strings of some celestial instrument!

What burning beds of heather bloom lie wasted,
  Save dusty bees with gold-bags wandering come,
Scenting afar fresh-minted gold untasted,
  Then oh! the deep-voiced traffic and the hum!

What deserts dark with gloom of thousand thunders,
  And earthquake's tread left visible in fear—
Dumb with the pauseless march of Nature's wonders,
  For ever hushed Heaven's still small voice to hear!

What soundless melody of light and shadow,
  In dumb procession journeying evermore!
What sunlit crests, and gleams of skyey meadow,
  Trod by no mortal, stretched by eagle's door!

What melodies of earth's unnumbered nations,
   Now struggling with her tears, shall yet ere long
Join in the chorus with unknown creations,
   And lift to heaven the majesty of song !

III.

Hail, primitive wild lands of peak and river,
   Nature's austere simplicities sublime,
Grand elemental wastes, where God the Giver,
   Godlike, comes down to sit with guests of Time !

What sudden splendours lighting up far valleys,
   What inspired moments startle the lone mere !
Unearthly rapture floods the pine-wood alleys,
   Dark tarns glance back half furtively for fear !

What mountain farms, that never knew a sickle,
   Hang perched remote on brink of lonely fall—
World-severed—save the redbreast's artless trickle,
   And breast of burning beech-leaf, links us all.

What thundering torrents light the deepening gorges
   With light of the thrice-sifted mountain foam !
What glorious passion, O ye battling surges,
   Thrills with heroic energy the gloom !

What bridal birch-groves, bright-haired moorland
    daughters,
  Dance in the dewdrops !—and in breezy haste,
Ah ! the sweet steppings of those silver waters,
  Glancing from stair to stair along the waste !

What worlds of pathos haunt this storm-rent planet,
  Where pensive generations wander late—
Oh ! the lost language of the riven granite,
  With none to spell the syllables of Fate !

RAINBOW SUNDAY.

On September 30, 1883, at Ambleside, we carefully watched a rainbow of unparalleled duration, lasting from eight o'clock in the morning till four o'clock in the afternoon. It retained an unbroken arch and full colour all the time, and merely moved eastward as the sun travelled westward.

I.

BRIGHT breathing there hour after hour,
From Fairfield lap to Brathay Tower,
The grand ethereal creature stood,
One flushed foot plunged in Rydal Wood,
The other dipped in Brathay flood !
Yes, strange to say, that selfsame Bow,
Slow shifting, slid from hill to hill
Eastward, yet motionless and still,
And lingered on the whole day through :

Till like far tones of some faint knell,
It died at last on bleak Wansfell.
But as it left the mountain's brow,
One said—recalling Heaven's first vow—
" God is gone up from talking now !"

II.

Keen Autumn breezes from the north,
With flying showers, first drew it forth ;
But what maintained it there all day,
Fair, lustrous arch, divinely gay,
The Rainbow-Lord alone may say.
For when the flying moisture ceased,
Still, still the rainbow ne'er decreased—
Though Fairfield's lap with sun brimmed o'er
Nor moisture fell of dew or shower,
That faithful Bow with fond impress
Still stained the crags with loveliness.
Heaven's Flower in blossom since the Flood !
Heaven's phantom storm-flower gracious, good,
That flying blossoms where wrath stood—
Eight hours at least that Sabbath day
The sacred symbol stood at bay,
Fresh garlanding those mountains gray !

SUMMER DAWN.

I LEANED against the lattice o'er the lawn,
  What time stars veil themselves from mortal eye,
  And watched, 'mid visible hush of earth and sky,
The pale virginity of summer dawn
Long lingering rapt! her sleep robes half withdrawn,
  Shyly, as if by unseen hands on high—
  When lo ! gold-girt with instant sovereignty,
She seized Day's flashing fire-reins, and was gone !
Down-sweeping luminous from height to height,
  With kindling skirts that made the vale sublime,
All Nature hushed, suppressed all glory-light,
  She lingered kneeling long that dewy prime—
Then, with one burst that flushed the infinite,
  Kissed back new colour to the cheeks of Time !

MOUNTAIN-TOPS.

Oн, hunger for brave singleness of heart !
   Here ranging through the vast, the terrible,
   Where mountain summits dim ascending dwell
And peer into eternity apart—
Where from dread solitude's stern centre start
   Far-flashing torrents, whose breeze-wafted bell
   Summons thee, with jagged crest and lonely fell,
To worship the I Am with all thou art !
Oh, hunger for brave singleness of heart !
   While Faith and Hope, dread spies, through upper
      air,
Climbing stupendous aisles of unhewn art,
   'Mid Nature's boundless hush of unformed prayer,
Start back surprised by man's dread counterpart—
   Earth's loftiest throne left sceptreless and bare !

ESKDALE.

O the wild torrent's sounding boulder bed !
　With　branching　fern-plumes　decked　like　desert
　　　king,
　Shadowed with birch-trees, fringed with purple ling.
'Twixt hills in pomp of amethyst outspread—
Here in life's singing highway, here, I said,
　'Mid cloistered coolness, as from crystal wing
　Whirled past me wet with every mountain spring,
'Mid tossing boulder-blocks I'll lean my head.

Thus, as I sat entranced below the bridge,
　Lo, through the arch I spied an inner shrine,
Where upper falls high flashing o'er a ridge
　Of steep crag, soundless as in vision shine—
Like the majestic, swift, white feet of God
Down Time's wrecked stair, when Love sought man's
　　　abode !

ABOVE THE IRWIN FALLS.

HAIL! tossing tempest of wild purple hills,
    All blown about with life-winds fresh from God,
    Glowing as though a thousand kings had strowed
Their burning Tyrian by the foaming ghylls!
Hail! mighty amphitheatre of peaks,
    Each throned in awful solitude apart,
    Yet closing sternly round us, till we start
Accosted by strange silence, though none speaks!

But why along yon summit, bend for bend,
    On misty elbows leans one moveless cloud?
      Ye breezy waterfalls, why chafe ye so?
    White bell-ropes of the hills, why clash so loud?
      They chime us in to worship, let us go—
Lured by their stormy music, we ascend!

DOCK TARN.

We climbed and climbed, then, raptured, spied at
    last
  A heather-muffled tarn engulfed in hills,
  Whose treasury of secret waters stills
With a strange stillness all that region vast.
'Mid Nature's sternest wastes how wonderful
  Yon horseshoe of fair waterlilies wild ;
  This fir-plumed islet, like some orphaned child,
Cradled on thy rude breast, high mountain pool !

But whence this scene's weird pathos ? Is't that here
  Eternity and Time together meet,
And commune undisturbed by this lone mere
  All day, till, warned by sunset's rosy feet,
The young moon, entering realms of sinless light,
Spreads wide the cabalistic scroll of night.

LODORE AFTER SUMMER RAINS.

CRADLED in mosses on the cloud-kissed fell,
Where drop by drop it grew inaudible—
Thence schooled 'mid boisterous moorlands, braced
    and free,
Singing its way to life and liberty,
The sky-born rill sets forth without a guide—
Time's own rude child-heart here personified.
With many a bubble-wreath in triumph worn,
And bold adventure of the wild inborn,
Swift through the heathery waste, where wandering
    late
The dusky grouse calls secretly her mate,
And the wild sighing of the mountain grass,
Drowsy with music, lingers loth to pass—

She fearless presses !—thence by bend and reach,
Babbling her artless elemental speech,
She winds from tarn to tarn, from inn to inn—
Wild Nature's hostels, where, escaped from din,
The mountain waters pause, thence start again,
Chiming a bright to-morrow in their strain,
On perilous journeyings downward to the plain.
Hark ! the light breezy voice flings far and wide
Her airy challenges on every side :
Now murmuring ancient secrets of the fells,
Deep and eternal ; now, like fairy bells,
From many a purple cleft and winding stair
Of rippling silver, haunting the blue air !
While the buff sunlit hawk, with sleepless poise,
Hunts the dim summer gorges without noise ;
And tall rays stalk with spiritual tread
The flushing heath or lonelier mountain head ;
Or glide in troops o'er many a gulf profound,
Gulfs of blue thunder-gloom, without a sound—
O'er whose high brink some quivering scarf of foam
Marks the black torrent's cleft and eagle's home.
Till now at length, green twilight of the wood,
Dancing with dappling showers of pattering gold,
Woos her blithe guest 'mid listening solitude
To hoary depths rock-strewn with altars old.

Thus from rapt childhood spent 'twixt heaven and
    earth,
Half dream, half song, the wild stream now bounds
    forth;
And unabashed, though heavens grow black with
    rain,
And the pale sheeted columns pace the plain,
Forth 'twixt stupendous portals of sheer rock
Rent wide asunder by convulsive shock,
But healed with living verdure, healed and crowned—
It bursts with proud pomp, thundering bound for
    bound.
Just then at mid-noon (sweet sign from on high!)
As the spent storm-cloud dark retreating lowers,
And flying chasms of rent sapphire sky
Span at a stretch those cliffs' gigantic towers,
Lo! the fair crescent moon's pale phantom face,
Journeying, stood still; and, pausing a brief space
Right in the gap above that jagged abyss
Where warring voices vex the wilderness,
Gazed down in silence! There, o'er that dread
    steep
With bared rent breast, plunged one vast thunder
    leap
Of roaring waters, shattered in their sleep—

Their quiet sleep unbroken on the fell
Now shattered !   Whence, white, swift, invulnerable,
Burst into life a hundred wild Lodores,
Launched headlong from a hundred foaming floors ;
Not one bold stream's huge twisted torrent dread,
Molten, convolved in one tumultuous bed,
But a majestic throng of glorious falls,
Bounding for ever 'twixt resounding walls—
Some pale with beauty of sublime distress
Veiled in the dust of their own brokenness ;
Some flashing forth forgiveness like the sun,
Screen in their fall the rocks they break upon ;
Others, before them hurling spectral spray,
Plunge to their doom, and ghostly pass away ;
While, starting into birth in pauseless flight,
Fierce crystal foam-sheaves, nodding plumes of light,
Charge onward, downward, maddening in their course,
Deep calling unto deep 'mid thunderings hoarse,
Till where black cataracts of boulders hurled
Headlong, yet poised—self-poised—against the world,
Still that triumphant throng of glorious falls,
Bounding for ever 'twixt resounding walls,
Sweeps on in proud procession of pale state
And robes of awful doom now dedicate—
Descending evermore, yet evermore
Descending, while moist shuddering banks adore,—

And toppling isles of storm-blocks riven and tost,
With wrecks of forest trees, whirl stunned and
  lost !
Thus o'er the fatal chasm instinct driven—
Instinct, the inviolable law of Heaven !
That headlong Flood (her flying death-robes rent,
No more to veil dread nature's sacrament)
Dared the white deed that in one single hour
Deliverance wrought, and filled the land with power !

Thence from that sounding sanctuary of awe,
Though none betray the mysteries they saw,
All perilous falls forgot and fury past,
The exultant flood expands a lake at last—
One broad o'erbrimming lake's bright reservoir
Of light, and life, and peace for evermore !
There the fringed shadowy marge with pencilled grace
Frames in deep bays Heaven's calm sequestered face—
There the blue heavens unveil themselves, and straight
All their pure sapphire soul communicate—
There pillowed on broad leaves in fairy creek,
Starred waterlilies lean their dainty cheek ;
There the white skiff that fearless courts the breeze
Hunts, and still hunts, sun-painted images.
For now no more that gulf of sacrifice,
Buried in green depths far from searching eyes,

Awes the bent ear of time with echoing death ;
But liberated now, triumphant Faith
Spreads her white wings in limitless delight,
And bending o'er proud Skiddaw's limpid sheet
Like fairy's magic pen inscribing it,
Still swift that white wing skims, till lost to sight,
With glittering keel the mirrored infinite !

BLEA TARN UNDER COLDBARROW FELL.

Half-locked within the mountain's lone recess,
  High on the fells a tarn secreted lay,
Before it tracts of boundless wilderness
  Stretched without limit toward the sinking day.
But now the tarn's dark depths grew chill and curled,
  Gray twilight threatened, when, as home we turned,
Late sunset broke and blazed against the world,
  And the huge mountain socket flamed and burned.

Dim peaks stood forth enlarged and glorified,
  Some, half-retreating, let the golden mist
Wrap their stupendous flanks from side to side,
  Others stood worshipping apart awe-kissed;
But one all spirit seemed, half prayer, half dream,
Its faint rose-flesh steeped in no mortal beam!

A LUNAR RAINBOW BY CRUMMOCK WATER.

Sudden o'er solemn mountain vale by night,
   Swift as to keep some unseen foe at bay
   Advancing stealthily on mortal prey,
Just as the full moon climbed storm-summits bright,
A startling vision broke upon my sight·—
   Broad, vivid, low, outstretched athwart the way,
   A lunar rainbow, swift that none could stay,
Her ghostly arch had planted left and right.

One pale foot firm on the dark trembling lake,
   One on weird mountain-side stood forth alone,
Like some bright breathing creature just awake,
   It stilled the hushed night with unearthly tone.
What awe and worship follow in her wake,
   When Nature works wild magic all her own !

THE HOME OF THE WATER-OUZEL.

Shut between mighty cliffs, yon desperate pass
    Still ever upward urges its blind way
Through treeless solitudes of mountain grass,
    Uncheered by mortal sound the livelong day,
Save burrowing under rocks now smooth as glass,
    Or now unfettered sparkling into play,
Wild sunlit waters, though 'tis Michaelmas,
    Lull silence into trance with dreamlike lay.

This is the water-ouzel's shy retreat,
    There in the torrent-bed from stone to stone
She noiseless flits ; then poised on steadfast feet,
    Dipping her dusk head, she trills forth alone
Love's sunniest, airiest gossip by her nest,
One milk-white foam-flake bound across her breast.

ST. JOHN'S IN THE VALE.

The dewy stillness of the sacred morn
    Still hallows stream and copse and shadowy well,
    While secrets of high Heaven inviolable
Faint breezes whisper to the bending corn.
Stretched 'twixt twin vales yon huge ridge, torrent-
        worn,
    Lifts, hid in its green lap high 'mid the fell,
    Prayer's lowly roof and ivy-mantled bell,
Whose echoing summons down each vale is borne.

A Druid's circle crowns the neighbouring height,
    Dark, mystic, weird—but vain its ruins lower
O'er that green spot of peace baptized in light—
    Time's verdict stands—Love, love alone is power,
The Tree of Life's broad shadow is man's home,
Hark, through the sunlit gates the nations come !

THE MEETING OF THE GHYLLS.

AT THE FOOT OF CRINKLE GHYLL, HELL GHYLL,
AND BROWNIE GHYLL.

NAY, go no further now—
Well may our footsteps linger awe-detained,
This is the very heart of loneliness—
All is primeval here—here let us pause,
And spend the rest of this long summer noon
'Mid Nature's own unguarded solitudes.
Here, where descending from huge craggy heights,
And dark o'erwhelming terraces of rock,
Through winding gorges deepening rapidly,
In crystal confluence met, three torrent-floods
Dash their tumultuous voices into one
Broad tranquil stream of harmony ;—and see,

Yon primitive rude bridge of wilding boughs,
From pier to pier of boulders rudely flung
Across the foaming waters, tempts our feet :
But as it trembles 'neath our cautious tread,
Mark with what rude skill shepherd hands have
        wrought
This wattled floor o'erlaid with moorland turf,
Making safe highway for the mountain flocks
That wander limitless these lofty fells—
Now this side, and now that, the perilous gulf,
But everywhere within these desert heights
Built in with incommunicable peace.

In such a spot as this I'd wish to die—
Here where the world is folded from my sight,
And blotted from remembrance like a dream,
And nought remains but barest elements
Of virgin rock and stainless waterfall—
Nature's own last wild austere sacrament
Of crag and torrent, bright o'er-canopied
With one broad seamless belt of bare blue heaven,
Deep and eternal—and on these alone
The soul feeds, and is satisfied and still.
'Twere easy to pass hence, methinks, unheard
Into the land of everlastingness,

The land of open vision and far rest—
And never more return to faithless dreams,
And din of human destinies half wove,
And wrecked halfway in weaving.
                              Ah ! brave world,
My spirit revels in this barrenness,
To me it seems the vestibule of heaven,
Death comes not here, for here is nought to die,
And nothing lives save deathless springs of life,
Born of the gathering waters from above,
Fed from eternal sources in the hills,
Winding from crag to crag with glancing feet,
White-winged and diamond-footed in the sun—
Careering down black channels of rent rock,
Or glassing stainless their blue slaty bed—
Aye squandering ceaseless music on the wild,
Like some white disembodied soul, all song,
That late returned to visit haunts of Time
And problems of past fate interrogate,
Comes dancing by, bright scattering evermore
Wild mirth and music round the hoary feet
Of solitude all scarred and seamed with age,
And hoar with mysteries of life outlived,
And memories of a dim and earlier world !

THE HARVEST-MOON.

(MATTERDALE CHURCHYARD.)

WHITE shepherd of far flocks of light,
That throng the gateways of the infinite
In grand allegiance to unwritten law,
Filling the face of darkness with proud awe!
Doth He who first wrote down in faith's bold hand
These noble characters none understand
Yet conscience trembles at in every land,—
Now draw forth from dread archives of the world,
'Mid banners of the universe unfurled,
Gray covenant-deeds of Harvest dews-impearled!

White shepherd of the crownèd year,
Thou visitest with thy celestial cheer
Earth's perfumed orchard alleys bending mute,
Spring's festive snow-bloom turned to ruddy fruit:

Thou cherishest the vines—the bursting grape
In purple ambush plotting rich escape :
Thy silver footprint, lighting everywhere,
Anoints with dews of sleep the busy air,
Like liquid bridal blossom dropping fair

White shepherd of pale dews and wheat
Up-piled in stooks of amber at thy feet ;
Each amber stook in attitude of prayer,
Kneeling as if for benediction there,
Seems steeped in floating mystery of light
Like breath of angels, spiritual, bright—
Each with its sleeping shadow by its side
Like some tired pilgrim crept from the world s tide,
Transfigured unawares, and glorified.

White shepherd of earth's harvest-field,
Lift high o'er earth thy broad dilated shield,
That, breathing lustrous forth soul-radiancy,
Lightens rude toil with Heaven's own solemn glee.
Once more descending stoop 'mid rustic bands
That glean belated now the yellow lands,—
Stoop shining shoulders through the infinite,
Gleaning last gold 'mid supernatural light,
That nought be lost in God's most holy sight !

White shepherd of the fells and rocks,
Thine the lone mountain fold and shadowy flocks,
That, heedless of wild creatures with bright eyes
Soft couched where dewy bracken thickest lies,
Range the entrancèd waste, the dim recess,
Where fountains bubbling in the wilderness
Track their own course in music and white mirth,
Girdling the antient crags and sleeping earth
With flashing amulets of magic birth !

White shepherd of the lakes and meres,
Thou, though thou dwellest 'mid the shining spheres,
Dost stately walk this rude untutored land,
Where solemn mirrors stretched on either hand,
Whether deep set in summits of the hills
Or stretched 'mid dreaming vales and glittering rills,
Crave passing glimpses of thy features fair,
'Mid wonder of white rain and blanchèd air,
And muse all night in rapt communion there !

White shepherd of the mountains hoar,
Down rugged steeps thou ceasest not to pour
The virgin transport of that sinless smile,
Hallowing each chasm dark and rude storm-sculptured
    aisle.

Thou pourest upon earth the stainless heaven,
Chaste, undefiled, 'mid nature gashed and riven,—
All broken things thou healest,—things bereft
Thou tendest, hence yon shining garment left
In the torn mountain side's dark wounded cleft !

White shepherd of the yew-girt sward,
White night of deathless innocence restored !
Yon heaving turf with its long mouldering guest—
Time's last frail billow held in green arrest,
Heaven's spirit-lips press shining, till the cold
Grass coverlet wraps fair the slumbering mould.
Eternity steals forth now Time's asleep,
Gable and porch their silver sabbath keep,
And dust renews Divine relationship !

TARN ON NAN BIELD PASS.

Scarce had we scaled the mountain's stern recess,
  And in its rugged lair at length descried,
  Hemmed in with towering cliffs on every side,
The lonely mate of crag and wilderness—
When from the stormy surface of the lake,
  A wild white whirling smoke of water-dust,
  Lifted and driven by each passionate gust
Of fierce winds down rock gullies, o'er us brake.

Far off, from fell to fell, in brimming haste,
  A winding chain of bounding waterfalls,
Startling with whiteness all that rocky waste,
  Clave ridge and black rift's heather purple walls
With virgin flash, as if from some pure sphere
God-life had o'erleapt mortal barrier !

MARDALE CHURCH, HAWESWATER.

Flanked by a roaring torrent from the fell,
  Girt with dark cloistered glooms of antient yews
  Whose purple wine-stained trunks strange awe
    diffuse,
Mardale's low shrine, rock-built, immutable,
Stands like the hills immutable around,
  That cast huge shadows self-reflectingly
  Into the lap of mightier hills than they,
Reared in stupendous stature from the ground.

The winding road that wanders by the lake,
  Elastic to its living influence—
The scented hay blue-skirted maidens rake,
  Where cranesbill's large blue eyes haunt marge and
    fence—
Yon flushed peak fondled by eve's last cloud flake—
  Ye touch my soul as with a spiritual sense!

WORDSWORTH'S ROUTE BETWEEN LOWTHER AND ULLSWATER.

WE call it Sceptre Lane,
  This high and leafy way,
For here the pale campanula
  Holds undisputed sway.

It winds o'er hill and dale,
  It touches on the moor,
It links the waters of the lake
  With Lowther's castle door.

Here sceptred spires of bells,
  Erect in stately ranks,
Like lamps of moonlit lavender,
  Light all the hedgerow banks.

But stay !—this is not all—
  Another spell is here ;
This way a pilgrim left the Hall
  For lonely Rydal Mere.

His spirit's touch remains—
  Not far from this he sung
A simple song of daffodils
  That thrills the English tongue.

He loved his native vales,
  He loved the glowing sky,
He felt the touch of Deity
  Rest on him from on high.

He lived his life alone,
  And yet his life survives ;
He left the world his solitude
  To people lonely lives.

The Poet's spell is here—
  We call it Sceptre Lane—
And here the pale campanula
  Shall never cease to reign !

ULLSWATER, FROM GOWBARROW PARK BROW.

DEPTHS of intolerable beauty—grand
   To ecstasy, break o'er this brow !—To advance
   Seems sacrilege—blue clefts of wild romance,
Lake, woodlands, lawns, a very fairyland
Lies outstretched like a dream on either hand,
   While Time's diviner bloom doth yet enhance
   The artlessness of nature's countenance,
Where veiled, unveiled, God's fair enchantments
     stand.
O colour, colour, love's last opulence !
   Thy universal language doth enshrine
The mystery of all magnificence,
   A supernatural ministry is thine—
These larger forms of speech doth God employ
To shadow forth His own unshadowed joy !

TO THE BISHOP OF CARLISLE.

My lord, within thy rocky diocese
   Thou hast a concourse of supreme delights,
   Thine are the wild hills with their towering heights,
Their gulfs of blue gloom and each purple crease !
Thine too the mighty torrents born of these,
   The seedling waters slumbering days and nights
   On moss and moorland :—thine all sounds and sights
Of flashing falls and murmuring inland seas !

Thine are the stately meres where at full length
   The mountains stretch themselves in sunset pride,
Weakness receiving their tumultuous strength
   And blending it with Heaven, till glorified
Mountain and mere, mute tarn, and torrent voice,
Sound it from vale to vale—Receive—Rejoice !

STORM ON THE HIGH FELLS.

Thus on and on we sped, from fell to fell,
  Higher and higher, till a thousand feet
And more we stood above the plain.   A spell
  Of mystery seemed round us passing sweet ;
For where the hills o'erlapped, as o'er each swell
  Burst fresh storm-vistas—thrice sprang forth to greet
Our menaced steps God's rainbow !—thrice to tell
  How love outruns the storm however fleet—
How grace pursues us though inaudible—
  How mercy dogs wrath down life's stormiest street,
Though none return with tidings—it is well !—
  How in that dread race which knows no dead-heat,
That race 'twixt Light and Dark urged fierce and fast
'Mid angel-watchers—Light cannot be last !

MOUNTAIN HOLIDAYS.

EARTH'S din dies here !   Unyoked, go scale the
    heights
  That climb and climb still heavenward evermore,
  Like grand blind hermit souls that seek God's
    door,
Unheeding how day's magic glory-lights
Hang their perpetual splendours on their sides,
  Or wandering veils perchance of phantom rain
  Like swift emotion pass and pass again,
Whispering life-secrets though no trace abides.

Go, but lest thou from God or Nature swerve,
  As morn first broiders priestly robes foam-white
With gold and sapphire, to go forth and serve
In lowliest ministry a waiting world—
  In prayer and praise go touch the Infinite
First, ere each day's joy-banner is unfurled !

AIRA FELLS, ULLSWATER.

O SHEETED azure, stretched from shore to creek,
  Nay, boldly say—magnificently swung
Suspended hammock-like from peak to peak !
  And ye wild waters, Nature's mother tongue,
Rippling exultant o'er your sapphire spoils
  Stol'n from the heart of heaven, and hidden there !
Such glorious moments crown creation's toils,
  Though cloud-swept cliffs look sternly unaware !

Here, dreamy rock glades, groves of ancientness—
  Divine neglect made pensive with decay ;
There, Boardale's green steeps, mountain fastnesses,
  Where ranging herds of wild deer to this day
Half swathed in tawny bracken antlered stand—
Oh ! ye bring back our grand grey Fatherland !

FUSEDALE BECK, MARTINDALE.

A SUDDEN bend and through the fell-farm gate,
  Just where the old mossed stone-steps mount the
    byre,
A gleam of waters made me hesitate,
  And forced my willing feet to wander higher.

Here, curtained in green alders like a bride,
  Now gushing her white heart out o'er the rocks
For very joy !—now trotting at my side—
  The fern-decked torrent burst through boulder
    blocks.

There, mighty hills give way to let her pass—
  The shy wild thing, first glancing from the moors !
Long that sweet voice lay lost in mountain grass,
  Now prattling like an inmate round our doors.

One deep dark cleft half tempted her to stay,
   All tapestried with cool green plants and flowers,
Which Nature fitted up in her rude way
   To give her time to gird her virgin powers.

But soon we met her sparkling down the glen,
   Her merry heart brimful of frolic speech,
Humming her plaintive fell tunes o'er again,
   Chiding and coaxing all within her reach.

Now trembling beds of juicy mimulus,
   Lured by her sunny smile, line either shore—
O Nature, what wild wealth and stimulus,
   What golden visions hast thou not in store !

Rich beds of green leaves succulent and soft,
   Crowned with such gold ! 'twould make a miser
       mute—
Whole bevies of gold slippers tossed aloft
   By revelling fairies startled by man's foot !

Hush ! No work this of sprite or water elf—
   Here, battling shiftless soils and torrent's drip,
Nature's grim earnestness betrays itself—
   One ruby drop stains each gold underlip !

Ah, happy wild stream !—her life's soon fulfilled,
   From this rock-knoll I catch the gleaming lake—
The deep embayed blue lake and one green field,
   The wooded steep, and white skiff's silent wake.

She left her crystal cradle on the fell—
   All the sweet sacred selfishness of home—
Those hillside sabbaths—hers the only bell !
   To give herself away all life to come.

'Tis well—'tis well ! Life-deeds are more than speech ;
   The sunset shadows soon shall throng the shore,
Soon the last keel shall grate upon the beach,
   And tired hands drop life's diamond-dripping oar !

TOURISTS CLASSIFIED.

THERE are four sorts of Tourists. The First " do "
    and dine,
Tear and stare, chew and chatter—active class this in
    fine.

The Second's the passive class—Tourists on tail,
Who *sit* through all beauty, by rail, mail, or sail !

The Third class, alas ! is the worst of the lot—
All labels, time-tables, note nothings ! yet blot
Reams of foolscap with jottings—all not worth a jot !

The Fourth class afresh from its Author receives
Nature's Book unadorned, letting God turn the leaves.

7—2

YORKSHIRE MOORS.

THESE moorland wastes are like a shoreless sea,
  Yon bare gray hamlet opening on the moor
  (The illimitable wild by each man's door!)
But adds a touch of human mystery
To these dim borderlands of Time; and ye,
  Weird groups of peat stooks, like rude huts of yore,
  Outstanding dark from orange bracken floor,
Tinge with rich gloom the vast infinity!

Yet the bee-traversed air is full of balm,
  And o'er the trackless moorland flames and burns
A mighty passion of wild purple—calm
  The boundless transport! Far as eye discerns,
  Ruby and amethyst now glow in turns—
The awe-flushed silence needs no other psalm!

MAN'S NEED OF CONTACT WITH NATURE

ONCE every year should all men touch again
   Their mother earth, and feel her mystic throb
Of universal sympathy and pain,
   Her secret soul-beat and her voiceless sob.
Thus linked with Nature's elemental reign,
   Felt 'mid the silence, men would cease to rob
The travelling centuries' majestic train
   Of faith and hope, and doubts would cease to mob

Man comes of Nature's lineage, and we live
   Daily by her allegiance, we aspire
To incommunicable heights, and strive
   To mount and mount—then suddenly we tire,
Dismount at death !—thus all men touch again
Their mother earth, and know themselves but men.

TURNHILL STONE ON THE MOORS.

Southward a moorland waste before us lay,
   Trackless save one tall mystic shaft of stone,
   Reared of old time to guide the wanderer lone
From moor to moor along his devious way.
But now the storm fell, and another shaft,
   A broken shaft of rainbow upright stood
   High on the moor—God's angel of the flood,
Absolving as he smote !   All Nature laughed—
Rich suppressed sunset light streamed wildly forth,
   Till o'er the startled, faded, moorland side
A festival of colour sprang to birth—
   Heaven's magazines of splendour bursting wide,
As though the surplus wealth of all the day
Were in one reckless moment poured away !

NEWWATH BRIDGE.

Tell me, wild bee, where doth the wild thyme hide
    By this rude gateway which I daily pass :
    Thou know'st untaught each scented blade of grass,
Nectar and honey-cell without a guide.
I love this foot-bridge, where the waters glide
    Clear, chestnut-coloured, chiming from the moor,
    I love each sapphire pool and amber floor,
Green dell and dimple—why am I defied?

"What is the knowledge for?" the wild bee said,
    "Work for the hive as I do, and you'll find
God gives us honey-dew as well as bread,
    'Tis only idleness that makes man blind.
Men have more sense than bees, but diligence
Is God Almighty's substitute for sense!"

WHEELDALE BECK.

HIGH purple moors stretch on without a bound,
   But where their sloping sides converge again
   A laughing beck comes tripping down the glen
With messages of life in every sound.
Gnarled birch and alder trees she babbles by,
   Bog-myrtle beds, rocks, rushes, blent in one—
   Then gambols onward, glittering in the sun,
Through purple wolds beneath a sapphire sky.

I crossed the moorland bridge, and stood and gazed
   Hither and thither with a wild delight;
Unspoken joy seemed everywhere.   I praised
   God's gifts aloud; but, ah! from out of sight
A startled grouse flew up on wounded wing—
Sorrow's romance still haunts each blessèd thing!

ROWAN-TREE FOLD ON THE MOOR.

Pause on this breezy eminence, and watch
   The sweet procession of wild waters glide
   From vale to vale ! A moment now they hide
'Mid arching coverts ; now burst forth to catch
Noon's sunblaze ; then blithe tripping unaware
   O'er stern rock steeps, they strike, not fire from
      flint,
   But virgin silver flashed from Nature's mint,
Copious as God's love spilt on doubt's dark stair ;—
Or like Spring's nested songbird none dreams nigh,
   When, startled by rude step, up ! rippling soars
   A wandering ecstasy of worshipping wings,
Sunlit, as touched with favour from on high,
   Till lost, re-lost, that wild fond heart outpours
      Such magic soul-lays, Toil stops, weeps, and
      sings !

THE FORD, OR FORGOTTEN INFLUENCES.

Dim unrecorded night-rains came and went,
  And morning broke o'er all things bright and new;
  Blue heavens poured down their unabated blue,
Green earth looked greener, lighted with content.
But when we reached the ford, where all her veins
  The laughing brook showed proudly yesterday,
  As, tired of rest, she plaited in her play
O'er pebbly shoals her amber locks in skeins,
All play was over !—tumult fierce and wild,
  A roaring wind of wings swept rudely by,
Floodgates were burst ; and as I stood and smiled,
  A mob of angry tongues, white hands flung high,
Defiance threatened ! Record still remains
In life, in death, of unrecorded rains !

THROUGH THE OPEN CHURCH DOOR.

Three sweet soul-vignettes Nature this year lent
   Her city child, sore prest on Sabbath morn :
   Once through a forest hamlet's church-door borne
Softly, 'mid hush of solemn sacrament,
The cuckoo's note with hum of wild bee blent
   Made spring-time in my breast. Again brain-worn,
   Northward 'mid mountain vales and summer corn
Soft winding Esk's hushed murmur's deep content
Stole in 'mid worship through the open door,
   Like tidings of a life that cannot die.
Then once again beside a purple moor,
   Prayer's western door flung wide, without I spy—
Loveliest of Sabbath pastorals—white flocks
Couched 'mid green sunny uplands and cleft rocks!

THE SEEN AND THE UNSEEN.

Blue distance veils the secrets of the mountains—
  Dim gorge and chasm, glimmering lakes and trees,
Moon-painted birch-stems by the shadowy fountains
  Glancing with flying tresses in the breeze.
And the dread silence of this world of ours
  Hides deep within its bosom all earth's din—
The Babel city's ceaseless clanging hours,
  The immeasurable sob of human sin.

And shall not heaven above us, silent, dumb,
  Far stretching upward, infinite and vast,
Hide in its fair depths jewelled city's hum—
  Love's mustering angel-armies' trumpet-blast—
Adoring hosts with folded wings of praise,
Or the swift-flying seraph's lark-like lays?

MODERN CULTS.

Humanity itself is some men's sky,
　　To leave their personality to earth,
　　Which thus through countless deaths works
　　　　new birth,
This, this is life's high destiny—to die !
Some in materialism find their heaven,
　　On science, nature, art, they lean and live :
They seize all God's gifts, save to be forgiven,
　　Then trespassing on God's prerogative,
They who at Nature's feet long groped and slaved
　　Dictate divinity to Deity,
　　Crave Christ to save them, but imperiously
Create the Christ by whom they will be saved ;
Till the last spark of Godhead left in dust
Fanned to a flame, they worship man's cold bust !

EXEMPLAR ONLY, OR EXPIATION ALSO?

WHAT means Christ's death?   Was He for sinners
    slain,.
  Or slain by sinners, and His life alone
  A glorious window lighting the unknown?
His death blank loss, or else man's richest gain?
And what to us is Christ's life, that fair life
  Reflected in four mirrors of the Word?
  Life's living lamp? or more—death's dying Lord?
Speak, mighty Son of God, and end the strife.——

"Were My whole life but to show man who failed
  The life of righteousness, I had not left
My life half writ, My death four times detailed.
  No life, sole writ for life's sake, were bereft
Of childhood, boyhood, youth, yea, manhood's
    bloom—
No, the ideal life were whole from birth to tomb!"

DEPRESSION.

Dread forger of earth's darkest links of fate,
   Most hellish foe of man, Depression drear,
   Still educating darkness year by year
To come at call and drape Heaven's bright estate
Then fascinating most when most we hate,
   Thou digg'st thine own abyss down which plunge,
   Absorbing all life's sunshine like a sponge
That darker grows for all its crystal weight !

Poisoning with thy fell breath like ruthless leaven
   The common light of life, the love, the cheer,
Thou photographest spirits unforgiven,
   Studying the death-cold science of a tear !
Stealing God's altar fire to scorch hope's wings,
Thou burrowest under blessings for new stings !

CRITICAL MOMENTS.

Mysteries of life which wondering years engage,
    Lost links, dark problems, changeful freaks of
        fate,
    Oft in one hour stand forth illuminate,
When Faith turns blindly o'er life's next page.
And the long wars with Nature which we wage,
    The slow intestine strife, the thorn, the weight,
    Oft one strong moment's reflex lustre straight
Invests with grandeur for all after age.

Has Heaven not granted to each living soul
    Some one apocalyptic moment bright,
When life's long panorama as a whole
    Bursts into magic outline on the sight,
All love-lit with God's purpose from the first?
Then seize the proffered clue, and end life's thirst!

HOPELESS IDEALS.

Nay, envy not the deeds of mighty men
  Because the partial Fates give thee no share :
Thou shar'st not their humanity in vain,
  And that a thousand spirit-links declare.
Bone of thy bone, the selfsame air ye breathe,
  Suckled at Nature's breast alike ye lay ;
Like spoils to both dead centuries bequeath,
  Both wear alike man's proud historic clay !

But deeds lack opportunity?   Then see
  At least in soul thou stretch thyself sublime
To the full height of their humanity ;
  Great men are but the mirrors of their time,
And each new wave's high towering jewelled crest
Is but one more proud sample of the rest !

THE STEAM-ENGINE.

Whence, self-impulsive being, hadst thou birth?
   Heaven's living sun begat, as sages tell,
The food by which thou livest, deep in earth
   Long ages hidden, and there spiced full well.
O spirit-king! when thou with mighty mirth,
   Freshed with deep draughts of wine from Nature's
      cell,
And flushed with sun-born food and fiery hearth,
   Dost rouse thee from thy lair at battle's smell—
Forth from thy forehead float live plumes of snow,
   Aye dying and aye leaping forth to life,
As with one shout, and but one glorious throe,
   Thou plungest proudly in the wingèd strife;
So heaven-eyed genius, with one glorious grief,
   One giant aim, doth time and space lay low.

THE MORNING SEA.

CRADLED in sapphire mist, Morn's sunlit Deep
    Wakes the whole world with laughter, darkness
        past,
    And with immeasurable music cast
Shoreward, 'mid sighs of strange relationship,
Earth's wandering mystic kinsman loves to keep
    Her ear attent on mystery to the last,—
    Whilst like sea-butterflies with wings shut fast,
White ships walk summer seas in stately sleep!
Here fondling mother-like the pink-lipped shell
    That pearly grot or bubbling fountain paves,
Rocking the cradle of the asphodel—
Yet all the while thou'rt thundering evermore,
    With multitudinous hosts of armèd waves,
Loud at the gates of Thule's utmost shore!

SHAKESPEARIAN SONNET DEFINED.

'Tis the upsoaring of a single thought
   Heavenward, in bright gyrations higher, higher,
   Like the first lark at dawn, all dew and fire,
Kindling and kindling with the glory caught
From day scarce risen :—'Tis a song unsought
   That, mounting of itself, doth swift aspire,
   Trembling with lustre of suppressed desire,
With lifting purpose winged, and music fraught.
When thus the octave sweeps aloft on high,
   The sestet hovering spreads forth sunlit wings—
Exultant moment ! then from ringing sky
   Drops softly down with joyous balancings.
The couplet now crowns all—no close like this—
'Tis love's own argument—rhymes clench that kiss

THE HEART OF STONE.

A mossy heap beside my pathway lay,
　So fresh and green, its swelling bosom bare
　Peeped forth into the sun and light and air,
Courting the balmy kisses of sweet May,
That from the eye of man it seemed to pray
　One look of love; or might it meekly dare
　The living pressure of his hand to share,
That warmth should be its life, its joy, its stay.
What heart could echo not that silent prayer?
　With tenderness I gazed upon that breast
Of silken moss—it sweetly waited there—
　So stooping down, with tenderness I prest
The mossy mound, but quick exclaimed, " Beware
　A stone may hide itself in Beauty's nest !"

BEACHY HEAD, SUSSEX.

Flanked with green downs the huge white chalk
    cliffs stand,
  Pure dazzling whiteness beetling o'er blue wave,—
  Here rent with chasms, there outstanding brave
Buttressed and jagged and carved as by rude band
Of sea-kings—or did Time's wild sculpturing hand
  These mystic strange sea-symbols there engrave?
  Whence innocent flocks of sea-gulls dive and lave
Snow pinions, or white paint the wet gold sand !

Thus on life's misty edges hoar with Time,
  Like white-winged children of the border-world,
Turning the stillness into awe sublime,
  On Faith's free flowing pinions bright unfurled,
Ripe souls launch forth to catch the eternal chime,
  'Mid deathless spray returning dew-impearled !

LEFT BEHIND.

I DREAMED a dream : In vain I strove to hail
  Song's mighty argosy, which at high noon,
  Launched   forth   in   splendour   on   Time's   wide
      lagoon,
Burned with rich blazoned pennon, silken sail ;
Whilst, seen afar exultant on the gale,
  Fame at the prow stood tiptoe—her wings shone
  God-like ! — steep pulsing shores flashed love-
      thronged—soon
Tossed their tumultuous farewells !   I stood pale.

Fast bound by carking cares till late that day,
  At length behind my cotton sail, that long
Shivered sedge-girt, unseen I stole away,
  Daring the silence with my freight of song—
When eve's long-lost glow glancing back, behold,
My cotton sail was turned to deathless gold !

SURREY HILLS.

EARLY SPRING.

ONCE more shy Spring veils in from vagrant eyes
   Tangle and copse, where music builds of old,
   And daffodils fresh pierce the virgin mould,
And Nature plots her annual surprise
Throughout a thousand leafy sanctuaries,—
   While sallow-buds mole-satin sheaths unfold,
   And honey-headed palms wave powdery gold,
And dust itself weaves living tapestries.
Yonder a garden sparrow sits upright,
   And with brown saucy bill reared boldly up,
Breasting a crocus barely its own height,
   Pecks the gold side from beauty's chalice cup !
While sudden Spring's inrushing spirit bright
   Wakes the whole world with one green wave of
      hope.

MEADOW DAFFODILS.

YE meadow children, that with dancing mirth,
  And airy minstrelsy of voiceless glee,
Stir dullard clod and furrows of old earth
  To psalm and song and wind-tossed ecstasy !
  First gospel of our childhood ! who but ye,
From winter's stern inexorable dearth,
Could fetch forth fountains of immortal birth—
  Death's burial-service chanted by the bee ?
Who else but ye, glad children, could inspire
  With your inevitable laughter-light,
From tier to tier, all Nature's deathless choir,
  Till star greets star far up the infinite—
Who else sow earth with Love's tumultuous fire
  Till dew and dust and deity ignite ?

THE WOODLAND CALL, NORBURY PARK.

Come, loiter through the leafy lanes with me
This blessed springtime, bright with dews impearled,
And drink the breath of cowslips with the bee,
And breathe again the morning of the world—
As if Creation were but yesterday,
And God Himself had only just withdrawn,
And still His footprint lay upon the lawn,
And still the deep wood-silence round Him lay—
Still through green cloistered aisle and dreamy brake,
And breathing space secreted at its heart—
Where fearless creatures deeper stillness make,
The awe of God's great silence held each part.
Here, folded in the mighty hills' embrace,
O'er-roofed with beech-grove's luminous green sleep,
Ere yet the noonday shadows trespass deep,
Fair lawns and uplands noiselessly we'll trace,—

And mark the mellowing woodland's earliest tints,
That melt in soft aerial bloom afar,
While loneliest cottage roof gives verdurous hints
How resurrection-life bursts every bar ;
And resurrection raiment spotless white
Each leafless blackthorn veils in virgin light.
Now all the teeming landscape laughs for joy,
Green-lighted woods smile deep with inward glee ;
Shade melts in shade with subtlest melody,
All earth now boasts one Master's proud employ.
Come, lend yourself to Nature for to-day,
And let her lead you through the blossoming May ;
Yea, list but lovingly, and she'll impart
A thousand secrets from her brimming heart—
Pause, and she'll make the singing silence seem
The supernatural murmur of a dream.
List ! through her living wheels' sabbatic hum
Faith hears the muffled tread of worlds to come !

MAYTIME IN SURREY.

O THE virgin step of the early dawn,
And the silver dews on the sleeping lawn,
And the heights of heaven given back to our sight,
And the ampler reaches of splendour and light,
And the spirit of life let loose o'er the world,
And the sovereign gladness o'er cloud and lea,
From the tender hope of the leaf unfurled
To the boundless health of the sapphire sea !

O the first spring breath of the eglantine,
First rapturous draught of woodland wine
Fresh wafted from dewy bowers, and bright—
Bright overhead far out-dazzling sight,
As through valleys I roam and umbrageous parks—
Oh, to pierce the o'erwelling fount of light
Through a wavering screen of warbling larks,
Till these glad eyes dance with the glory-sparks !

O the festive snows of the hawthorn bowers,
And the meadows all damasked with dappling flowers,
And gold cowslips pale by the hoary fence,
And groves dream-laden with innocence ;
While tangle and copse and each topmost bough
Is music-haunted, and bare liquid sky
Breaks forth into song o'er the cornfields now,
And the breezes of God go rippling by !

And the waters have caught a daintier tone,
And the moss is greener upon the stone,
And each bosky dell has its listening ears
And gambolling loves and shadowy fears ;
And the pheasant crows and then bursts away
Into denser depths of the pathless wood,
Where a thousand wild homes keep holiday.
And all is sunshine and gratitude.

And yonder, 'mid tangle of grasses and dew,
Where the hanging copses break open to view,
Lo, secreted a glory of hyacinth mist,
That with rose campions flushed turns to amethyst !
And dusk swallows skim th' o'er-arched river's face,
Whose fresh swoll'n current glides noiselessly by,
Half muffled in low sweeping chestnuts' broad grace,
Lifting white candelabra-like blossoms on high.

O the lilac bowers by the homesteads old,
And laburnum clusters like grapes of gold,
And the nestling cots veiled in leafy screen,
And the emerald flush o'er the village green ;
And the deep, deep lanes with their scented limes,
And blue masses of eye-bright clustering there,
And the hamlet tower with its antient chimes,
And the screaming swift in the upper air !

O the thousand spring tints of the forest leaves—
From the young tender drip of broad chestnut eaves,
And green russet-gold of the sunlit oak,
To the larches' soft fleecy verdure like smoke !
While cradled in glooms of the woodland deep,
The dove, with her great wooing heart in her throat,
Pours wave upon wave as in audible sleep
Love's one muffled murmur's prolonged wedded note.

But hark ! of all beauty this, this is the best,
That the bountiful earth which kept pent in her breast
Mighty yearnings hid long, now that sunshine and
      cloud
With their subtle spring voices are calling aloud,

Like an angel of hope has leapt up wide awake
In new might from her sleep, and her tense teeming
    soul
Sends up one wide murmur thro' bird, bush, and
    brake,
Till all Nature stands forth one vast life-breathing
    whole !

O the orchards deep muffled in bridal bloom,
And the gay linnets rifling each bowery room
Of white cherry, or pear, or apple rose red,
May's own dainty blushes and blossoms just wed !
Whilst hoar forest aisles dark columned and grave,
Where the blackbird talks love in his half-human
    tone,
Now that sunshine has flooded green transept and
    nave,
Ripple out into laughter—spring laughter—breeze
    blown !

O the joy to greet in the depth of the land,
'Mid Nature's lone voices and visions grand,
Some merry wee maid decked with childish ring
Of beads on her hand like a wedded thing,

Bubbling over with innocent merriment great,
(May wedding-ring never weigh heavier there !)
As she rides a-swing on the forest-gate,
Her bright eyes ambushed in sunny hair !

O the haunts, wild haunts, of earth's nameless
    things !
How they start from the dust as on blossoming wings,
Warm impassioned wings set with jewelled eyes,
Bright escutcheoned with breathing heraldries,
Like some fairy spirit half angel, half flower,
That hovers and floats and then flutters away—
Childhood's dreams of beauty come true every hour,
And old earth, blossom-blind, keeps creation's birth-
    day.

O the rippling roofs and the woodland halls,
And the sunny ridges and sapphire walls,
Where the stainless heavens exulting stand,
Like eternity girdling all the land !
And the woods keep sabbath from week to week,
And entangle in worship the trespassing breeze,
And the lights and shadows play hide and seek
'Mid the lawns and ancestral silences !

And the bees still murmur their old-world tale,
And the squirrel skims lightly the mossed park pale
And the cuckoo's note seems to mellow the air,
Though there's never a ghost of a sound left there.
And the gilded thickets are tipsy with light,
And the reeling saplings they laugh outright,
While innocence starts from each sinless lair,
And the soul goes forth to the infinite.

And leagues of bright buttercups gleam as of old,
Clad in Nature's own homespun cloth of gold,
And white butterflies waver from bower to bower,
Like the snowflake come down to wed with a flower
And each coppice and brake in this sea-girt isle,
Where sheets of blue hyacinths dreaming lie,
Seems a magic pool of forsaken sky ;—
And the world lives still in the Master's smile !

SPRING COWSLIPS.

Fʀᴇsʜ from the country, just this moment come !
   Hail, brimming basket of gold cowslips, wet
   With glistening meadow dews, and round them set,
Teeming with odorous breath that makes one dumb
For very blessedness like wafts from home,
   Lo, luscious clumps of purple violet
   (While dreams and odours blending tears beget)
With breath of the immortals fill the room.
O God, how rich this world is with Thy life !
   Where'er I go I stumble upon Thee—
The groves with psalm and canticle are rife,
   Unwritten scriptures teem in all I see ;
New winds of Pentecost wake leafy strife,
   And cloud and clod breathe immortality.

APRIL.

List, April buds are climbing up the gloom !
  Their colours folded fast like bannered powers
  Marching in secret, till, lo ! magic bowers,
Bursting their ambush, bring back our lost home.
The dark-winged war-clouds that seemed charged
    with doom,
  Like shrouded squadrons riding down the hours,
  In falling turned to soft baptismal showers,
And Winter's battlefield bursts bright with bloom.
Ah ! welcome Spring's rich caravanserai—
  Travelling from distant lands without a sound,
They come, they come, bright nomad tribes so gay,
  In gorgeous groups, from regions long ice-bound—
Reconquering earth with resurrection tread,
They fill the world with music from the dead !

BETCHWORTH BRIDGE.

EARTH, new-born earth, most antient, ever new !
    Exultant on this hamlet bridge I stand,
    Eyes, heart, both full—spring's fresh green fairy-
        land
Sun-smitten brings lost Eden back to view !
Here, wooded banks steeped in low level light
    Build, depth on green depth, dream-towers in the
        flood,—
    Fretted like finest file, there, shimmering brood
Spots of flawed crystal, breeze-whipt, steely bright.

But turn, and, lo ! bank-moored an islet fair
    Of leaning alder-trees juts out midstream,
Meadows afloat with royal gold are there,
    High waves of billowy foliage bound my dream ;
While shy coots from reed coverts at my feet
Lead forth their small dusk velvet downy fleet !

SUNSET IN A SURREY LANE.

" ALL heads uncovered in God's temple aisle !—
　　This is God's minster, though by human hands
　　Unwrought,—this proud high-vaulted arch expands
God-built !" thus spake the pastor with a smile.
The cuckoo's soft shout haunting our fair lands
　　Came blown about the arched and pillared pile,
　　And gold-robed sun-gleams in and out the while
Plied noiseless ministries Faith understands.

Spring had just finished her delightful toil,
　　No sound of axe or hammer had been heard ;
No débris fell, no scar remained to spoil,—
　　When suddenly, 'mid chant of bee and bird,
High-fretted roof, breeze-swayed leaf curtains fine,
Stooped　glory - charged,—God　filled　the　burning
　　　　shrine !

NIGHTINGALES.

Stopt in broad daylight 'mid the open copse,
  Stopt by a merry gang of nightingales
Flushed as with woodland wine !—my stirred heart
    stops—
  What would ye, jocund bandits of our vales ?
Spring's sweet intimidation still assails
  The ears of young and old ! though science lops
Time's rich growths,—flouts our hedgerows, sickles,
    flails,
  We still retain green thickets and hill-tops.

'Tis strange chance music squandered on the wild
  By unseen leafy tenants of a nest
Should make the mighty sage once more a child,
  Love-plundered of his heart-cares like the rest.
None draws from toil-worn feet the rankling thorn
Like some shy song-bird cradling her first-born !

WOTTON CHURCHYARD IN MAY.

High on a lawny ridge sloped toward the vale—
    Sweet landing-place on Nature's gradual stair—
'Mid elms embowered, God's sanctuary I hail,
    Hallowing the hush of sunset into prayer.
No sound disturbs the stillness of the dead,
    One thrush pipes clear his vesper hymn hard by,
'Mid lengthening shadows, on man's lowly bed
    Day lays his golden sceptre down to die.

Yon antient thorns that crown the pensive slope
    'Twixt giant beech-trees stand white swathed in
        bloom—
Ah, bridal daughters of eternal hope,
    Ah, virgin sentinels that watch the tomb,
From Time's worn sheath at death's consummate
        hour
Bursts immortality's transcendent flower!

SURREY HILLS IN SPRING.

Bright hang the beech glades quick with spring's
      young blood,
  A magic mist of hyacinthine flame
Floods sloping floor of copse and underwood
  With skyey vapour—haunts too shy for fame.
But one blue shadow pensive seems to brood
  Apart, as if some heaven-winged messenger,
  Pausing mid-flight and stretched enamoured there,
Sky-cinctured slept, and, breathing, awed the wood.

Oh for a year of living leisure time
  To study God's grand old green dewy book
Of Nature, with its heaven-blue clasps sublime,
  And dazzling gold sky-corners none may brook—
Till the whole soul within the man should burn
With kindling converse, and God's mystery learn !

OKEWOOD CHURCHYARD.

WHAT fruity notes are these ? what woodland wine
  Wakes liquid bubblings till the nightingale
  Whets all her love-powers ?—piercing swells love-
    pale
That long low indrawn whistle half divine !
Yea, quaff yet once more, lest your soul should pine,
  Last wafts of cowslip perfume on the gale.
While bending broom from coppice and park rail
  Waves her resplendent gold fleece towards June's
    shrine.

Now cross the foot-bridge,—on this grassy steep,
  Where in the green heart of the silent wood
Spring sits and spins for those that round her sleep,
  An antient fane for centuries has stood.
Veiled leafy pathways lurking everywhere
Link hermit homes with this lone House of Prayer.

AN EVENING RAMBLE IN MAY.

MAY, apple-blossom May ! whose bosom teems
  With new-born blisses bursting lids of dew,
  And joy-lit clusters, lighted through and through
With dreamlight that impoverishes our dreams—
What joy beneath thy sun's last level beams,
  At some delicious pause 'mid converse true,
  To stop and disentangle ever new
Sweet woodland voices blent with falling streams, —
Aerial lark high poised in sunny air,
  Like angel voice half lost within the Veil ;
  Soft cuckoo, thrush, low gush of nightingale,
Soul-ecstasies that melt the heart in prayer !
While the long wold's low cloud-ribbed roof of gold
Twixt flaming rafters burns, fold crimsoning fold.

SUMMER MOONLIGHT.

THE mighty landscape of the midnight Heaven
　　Breaks open noiseless on my raptured gaze,
　　Where evermore upon her shining ways
The immortal pilgrim of the sky is driven
In beatific quest of souls forgiven—
　　To lure by Night's white silver sabbath days
　　And lustrous silences to nobler praise—
Now day is done, and earth's last bonds are riven.
The unfallen world above us, stainless, pure,
　　Paved with snow-fleeces drenched with shining
　　　　dews,
　　Since Eden's gates first broke the fiery news,
Doth aye with her white sinless peaks endure—
To woo us back to immortality
Through Death's dim sleeping realm and lighted sky !

NATURE MASSING HER COLOURS.

First, snowdrop belts and unfurled daffodils,
    Like daintier snowdrifts flanked with flagon gold,
    To barren orchard aisles the news have told ;
And primroses rush out by pools and rills
And flood the banks, till every nook reveals
    Dew-tangled moonlight sleeping ! Blackthorns bold
    Bloom-muffled, milk-white, tempt hoar hawthorns
        old
To keep love's bridal o'er green vales and hills !

Blue hyacinths in sheets crowd up the copse,
    Orchards' soft billowy bloom begins to blush,
Rich buttercups spill gold that never stops,
    Warm poppy flames scorch cornfields with their
        flush ;
Last, to crown all, brave gorse and heather bands
Camp out for miles and fire the desert lands !

A SILVER WEDDING.

Five-and-twenty years ago,
 Mary, thou wert first my own,
White thy bridal as the snow,
 White thy spirit as the Throne.

Oh, the rapture of that vision !
 Bright soul-gleams 'mid sunny hair,
Meekness veiling love's decision,
 Dewy dawn's reserve still there !

Those were days of wistful wonder,
 Hope's fond halo o'er us both ;
Time has rent the veil asunder,
 What remains ?—diviner troth !

Never have I seen a life
 Simpler, nobler in its aim,
Steadier in the daily strife,
 Daily riper, yet the same.

Never have I known a love
  Purer, brighter from its rise,
Selfless as the souls above,
  Rich with wordless sacrifice;

Never knew a love so deep
  For all God's creation fair,
Patience to observe and keep,
  Thoughtful reason to compare—

Memory that long recalls
  Flash of wayside flower or star,
That like ripe fruit soundless falls
  In God's orchard grounds afar;

Love majestic and minute
  For all creatures great and small,—
Rustic song or strolling lute,
  Love's fine ear transmutes them all.

Never saw I faith so high
  In the everlasting Lord,
Courage to believe Him nigh,
  Courage to accept His Word;

Faith that nothing can destroy
  Coupled with sublimest fear,
Faith all confidence and joy,
  Faith behind the brimming tear ;

Faith on soberest reason based,
  Faith that with the thinking mind
Life's dark problems long has faced,
  Yet trusts God and human-kind.

Often when my soul was vexed
  With the conflict of the schools,
Thy swift instinct, unperplexed,
  Pierced the mist of wordy rules,—

Caught the eye of Truth afar,
  Undistracted by the crowd
Of fierce factions waging war,
  Rival lovers wrangling loud.

Was there any danger nearing,
  Thou didst pioneer in prayer !
Was hope's bright star reappearing,
  Thou didst haste to meet it there.

I have found thee—oh, how often !
   Sitting in thy room alone,
Dumb lips pleading, whilst eyes soften
   Rapt in converse with the Throne.

Ah ! the dark days and long illness,
   Weary feet on midnight floor
Battling death amid the stillness,
   Thyself half inside death's door.

Thou art all my earthly treasure,
   All my heart is lodged in thee ;
From thee life hath learnt her leisure—
   Its deep peace eternity.

Five-and-twenty years have passed,
   Mary, yet these eyes confess
Morn's first dews still nobly last,
   Mellowing years more richly bless.

Hand in hand, brave Mary mine,
   Speed we toward the soundless sea ;
Wafts of seaweed and the brine
   Brace the spirits of the free !

Richer clusters all the way
    Pluck we as we near the sea,—
Life or death, take what ye may,
    Ours is immortality !

THE POET IN INVOCATION.

O Father, Holy Father of my soul,
Who of frail Time hast builded for Thy Son
This mighty dwelling-place, with light inlaid,
And life inwoven with the meanest thing,
And brooding over all love's hallowing wing—
Take, Lord, mine hand, I'm but a wayward child,
And nothing know save that I fain would hide,
Show me the wonders Thine own hands have
      wrought—
Thy six days' handiwork so wonderful,
And all their hidden wisdom. Let me spell
Thy words and works together. Lead me forth
In Thine almighty footprints yet once more
With eyes unveiled and spirit tablet white,
And memory, listening angel, at my side !
Lord, the strong spirit anchored at Thy feet,
Fain following Thee in ways past finding out,

Oft stands upon the brink and feels the awe
Where God's great silence listens to be felt !
Then, when the eye again reverts to earth,
How overwhelming is simplicity—
Where tiny pulses from God's mighty heart
Beat in each bush, and joy is daily bread,
And innocence still serves Him without fear,
And love and law are instincts 'mid the leaves.
And, oh, what wealth of happiness is Thine !
Who'st lodged the cheerful spark within the flint
And lit with joy the pebble's jewelled breast,
And hid a kindness in the sweet-brier leaf,—
Who, from the gladness of the morning sea,
Which like a mighty garment full of treasures
Casts forth the streaming sunrise on the shore,
Even to the dust that dances in the beam,
Hast shed the sense of beauty over all—
Beauty, the music of the voice of God
Adhering still to all created things !
And, oh, what depths of tenderness are Thine—
Who from Thy glorious goblets, sun and moon,
Pour'st forth unbidden wine and milk of light,
Rivers of grace which flow by each man's door :
And who, of joy's infinitude, Thyself
Hast erst implanted in the breast of all

Young creatures, as they enter into life,
The one glad impulse of wild gambollings ;
As men should bind a colt with blossoms first,
And harness it with garlands for a yoke !

O Thou great silent God, pervading all,
Thyself free Nature's fair beatitude,
Who—in the eternal vigilance of love,
From dawn's first golden signal o'er the hills
Waking the slumbering outposts of the world,
Each radiant leaf fresh damasked with fine dew,
To eve's last sunset beam that paints the fell
With retrospective glances of fond fire—
Thus, thus hast sent forth love to light us home,
Our feeblest thoughts may climb to Thee unheard,
A single thought may be Thy tabernacle :
So may we draw Thee down into our hearts !

O store up God's great love within thy soul,
So suffering never shall exhaust thy joy,
So darkness shall but draw out star by star
God's mercies, till the lap of Heaven o'erflows
With waiting worlds of light the sunshine hid !

THE FIRST SNOWDROP.

What name is thine in heaven, thou simple flower,
　That thus with trembling form, and forehead bent
　So timidly, like some pale penitent
Art first to greet me at my New Year's door?
And hast Thou then remembered, gracious Power,
　To wake this tiny creature from her tent
　In the cold earth, where, slumbering innocent,
She heeded not the sun, or dew, or shower?

By what name didst Thou call her long ago,
　When first she heralded the infant year
With silent salutation, that even now
　She duteous blossoms 'mid a world so drear?
Heaven's name for thee I know not; this I know,
God calls thee, and thou hearest, drop of snow!

THE THRUSH.

Hush !

'Tis the full-hearted thrush;

How calm

When the winter's sun burns red and low,

In the orchard where the snowdrops blow,

He mellows in the sunset glow

His psalm !

Hush !

'Tis the first melting gush,

Then slowly—

In notes by all of earth untaught,

Each tone it seems a liquid thought,

He pours rich meanings all unsought

Most holy.

Hush !

When the ripe warblings rush

And thrill,

Sudden 'mid wrestlings of delight

A pause ! as storm-clouds break, and bright

A lake of heaven's blue summer light

Hangs still !

Hush !
"Twas the same liquid crush,
Each stroke—
Far opening into that full heart,
Which would its very self impart,
And consecrate with life its art,—
Love spoke.

Hush !
Soft steal by yonder bush,
And gaze,
How broad that pale-brown speckled breast
Swells in soft fulness towards the west !
Its very being cannot rest
For praise !

Hush !
Fresh 'mid eve's fading flush
That voice
All song, and suppled by the dew,
With tremulous flute-notes wakes anew
Delicious challenges,—Ah ! few
Rejoice.

THE FIRST BEE.

Hark, the wild bee !—
    Humming through the air
Snatches of last summer's glee !
    Little merry murmurer !

Hark, the wild bee !
    Hush, there's not a stir !
Little talk at meals for thee,
    Little busy banqueter !

Hark, the wild bee !
    Prythee do not fear,
Every blossom blesses thee,
    Little pleasant plunderer !

Hark, the wild bee !
    Gold bags, I aver,
Slung from either thigh !—Then flee,
    Little moneyed messenger !

Hark, the wild bee !
    One in Heaven doth steer
Thee, far ranging hill and lea,
    Little vagrant voyager !

THE FIRST DAFFODIL.

FIRST spring daffodil,
Ribbon leaves flap o'er the rill,
Buds peep out with golden bill.

First spring daffodil,
Gaily toss your yellow frill
By the rushing water-mill.

First spring daffodil,
Little children soon shall fill
Tiny aprons at their will.

First spring daffodil,
Though the March winds whistle chill,
" I will blossom, that I will,"
Frets the pouting daffodil !

First spring daffodil,
Ever, ever, come what will,
Cups of sunshine rudely spill,
Pretty pouting daffodil !

THE FIRST WHITE BUTTERFLY.

Thou too a mortal, floating butterfly !
  My fellow-flutterer in the web of Time,
Wafted from hope to hope in search of joy,
  Winged breath of snow beneath the blue sublime !
Thou wert a worm, they told me, trailing low,
Whence these soft wings, then, trembling breath of
      snow ?
    " Asleep upon the dewy earth,
      Within my dusky cell,
    A yearning stirred me like new birth,
      And woke "—a spirit !   Blessed parable !

THE FIRST COWSLIP.

  Cowslips of Spring !
From your fairy may-poles juicy and pale,
And tassels of yellow bells scenting the gale,
    Swings the wild bee murmuring !

    Cowslips of Spring !
Asleep or just waking 'mid curtains green,
Milky buds lurk in the meadow-grass keen,
    Nestling low in a moonlit ring.

Cowslips of Spring !
From the wine-stained lips of your freckled cups
Honey and milk the brown nightingale sups
    To melt the heart of his mated wing.

Cowslips of Spring !
With clusters of joy ye light our lands,
And we gather your fragrance in our hands—
    Beauty and fragrance blossoming.

Cowslips of Spring !
Though the world grows old with sorrow and care,
There's eternal freshness in the air,
    The gladness of God to earth *will* cling !

THE CLOUDS.

And ye are tameless still, celestial clouds,
That all day long spread at the feet of God
Your glistering garments, silent in delight,
Too near His glory to give utterance—
Yea, God's own floor still roofs our fallen world !
Tameless ye shall be ever, wingèd throng,
For He who crowned man king of His bright world

In His own hands still kept your delicate reins,
And none may touch them but His gentleness,—
He slips around you His soft leash of light,
And leads you captive at your own desire !
I thank Thee, O my Father, for this love !
And I who never saw earth's mountain thrones
Fleeced with snow silence, see heights more sublime,
Pile towered on pile like mute eternities,
Resting their solemn peaks in God's near gaze.

And I who dwell far from the ocean's roar
May trace your cavernous cliffs' precipitous steeps
Fretted with foam, impending in blank gloom !
And I whose dreams are with the darkness chased
Uplift mine eyes where dreams more glorious far
Floating in voiceless vision over all—
New miracles to unknown harmonies
Melt each in each spontaneous and for ever !

And when the setting sun on golden shoals
Seems stranded, sinking like a flaming wreck,
Up the horizon ye in colours play
Unuttered anthems of adoring praise,—
Vast visible songs of victory, for death
Is but the sunrise of another world !

THE SKYLARK.

I.

Thy pitcher of full praise
Upbearing steadily,
In eager haste
That none may waste
Right into heaven upflee !
And now within the blaze,
With still undazzled gaze,
Oft spilling as it sways,
Clap over it thy little wings for glee :—
Love's pitcher filled below the sod,
In gratitude for one nest clod,
There empty at the feet of God.
Up, wingèd voice ! up, quivering heart of light !
And, climbing, kiss the glorious Infinite,
His garment's golden hem who reigns far out of
    sight !

II.

Oh, could I find thy ladder,
  I too would climb the sky,
And thence would pour forth gladder,
  Far gladder hymns of joy !

My song should far out-travel sight,
And love should take the wings of light.
But though I may not climb the air,
Behind the light's a secret stair
Worn by the noiseless feet of Prayer.

———✦———

THE RAINBOW.

"I do set My bow in the cloud, . .   and I will look upon it."—GEN. ix. 13, 16.

I.

My God, is this Thy bow?
　What must Thine arrows be?
Thy bow so richly dight
With varied skeins of light
　Spans earth and sea.
What arrows, then, in holy strife
Leap forth from Thee but shafts of life!

I gaze upon it now—
　That breathing burning sign,
Arched stream and mountain brow
　Become an instant shrine!

Dark storm-clouds rent depart,
    Blue heavens have purged their stains,
The bow still bent at Heaven's own heart
    Emptied—alone remains !

II.

Sweet refuge 'mid alarms,
    Ah, I do love thee well ;
These are the everlasting arms
    That ever round me dwell.
Between the sunshine and the cloud,
Between the guilty and their God,
O rainbow-wreathed, long hast Thou stood !
The Throne of Light itself's enthralled
In rainbow wreath of emerald.
'Mid heaven's own burning heart of blue
What spot betrays such gracious dew—
What dazzling summit half so fair,
The green, the green of earth is there !
And though no primary colour this,
    By alchemy that ne'er grows old,
    Heaven's alchemy of blue and gold,
Here faithfulness and glory kiss !
Yea, most of all I love to see,
To-day and in eternity,
What God is gazing on with me !

ON THE DEATH OF A FAVOURITE PONY,

WHOSE DEATH WAS CAUSED BY A WOUND INFLICTED
BY A PITCHFORK THROUGH THE CARELESSNESS
OF A STABLE-BOY.

One limb hung wounded by his side,
And thus he stood and stood and died,
My beautiful, my human-eyed,
        My Pony.

*   *   *   *   *

Who else but Death had heart to rob,
Without a sound, without a sob,
Thy castled limbs, my gentle cob,
        My Pony?

Thy coal-black eye so beaming bright,
Thy milky mane all tossing light,
Thy flowing tail's pure wealth of white,
        My Pony.

Thy polished knees of ebon black,
The quiet strength of thy meek back,
Fleet comrade, such as few could track,
My Pony.

Thy pricking ears caught every hint,
Thy eager hoofs oft flashed the flint,
How many a road still bears thy print,
My Pony!

Or sauntering through the lanes of spring,
Thy nose found home in everything,
Deep weedy bank or wayside spring,
My Pony.

Whene'er my steps approached thy home,
Thine eyes spoke eloquently, Come,
Alas, that God had made thee dumb,
My Pony!

Dumb friendship I could ne'er withstand,
The very silence makes it grand,
And draws my heart into my hand,
My Pony.

And if I stood beside thee long,
And cheered thee with a word or song,
Thine appetite came doubly strong,
     My Pony.

No juicy leaf the neighbourhood round,
Or cooling grass, but it was found,
And healing herb to make thee sound,
     My Pony.

We nursed thee with a mother's skill,
Anticipating thy dumb will,
And hope grew strong, but thy pulse still,
     My Pony.

I grudged the remnant of thy breath
Spent groping for the gate of death,
Which all too easy openeth,
     My Pony.

In the dark night thou diedst alone,
None heard thy fatal final groan,
Thy pillow the relentless stone,
     My Pony.

Roaming through some celestial pasture,
The wanton wound, the foul disaster
Forget, but not thy friend and master,
                              My Pony.

The whole creation groans aloud,
Man wraps glad nature in his shroud,
Then stalks a king above the crowd,
                              My Pony.

Too close, alas! are we allied,
Dumb labourers toiling at our side!—
Thy sinless sorrows broke my pride,
                              My Pony.

May He all wise, who did ordain
That life's mysterious link of pain
Guilty with guiltless should enchain,
                              My Pony—

Now teach me what mysterious grace
Cast the dark shadow of our race
O'er thy dumb, unoffending face,
                              My Pony!

THE FIRST SWALLOW.

Swallow, that with forkèd flight,
Like an arrow through the light,
Darting, diving, dazzlest sight,
      Sipping silvery sounds—

Skim again the sky-blue pool,
Just behind the village school,
Striking from the crystal cool
      Flashes of pure light !

Now the spring is fully come,
And no woodland leaf is dumb,
Happy hang your little home
      Upon my chamber-wall.

Gathering round thee thy twin brood,
Sift the summer light for food,
Guarded by man's gratitude,
      Guided from afar.

Breaking wild from gates of morn,
As of heaven's own brightness born,
Dash into a sea of corn
          Sweeping noiselessly !

Swift through every orchard-bough
Fearless shoots thy silken prow,
Nought of dust and din know'st thou,
          Ever-gliding gleam !

Now the primrose leaves the lane,
And the glowing campions stain
Fern and bluebell, back again
          Glance thy under-wings.

Living ever on the wing,
Though thou dost not soar or sing,
Yet thou art a blessed thing
          Slipping through the light !

Smooth as face of swiftest stream,
Subtle as its silvery gleam,
Busier than the brightest dream,
          Joy thy only praise.

THE FIRST CUCKOO.

O WELCOME, welcome, happy bird,
That out of stillness seemed to start !
There's something human in that word—
A human voice from nature's heart.

O welcome, welcome, happy voice,
That in a moment at my side,
Constrained from far by secret choice,
Announced itself without a guide.

The simple pathos of thy speech
Is more than music to the wise—
Record of reason none can reach,
Of science taught beyond the skies.

Year after year, whate'er may be,
Whate'er may change, thou art the same ;
Spring's tender immortality
Revives the freshness of thy name.

The year had gone, the world had died,
Again all living things rejoice,
As naught had intervened, replied
From the same spot the selfsame voice.

The mystery of that mellow call
Which floats unseen from tree to tree,
His Voice who moves unheard through all
Has softly summoned o'er the sea.

The message lodged within thy breast
Comes and withdraws at His command,
Whose instinct of sweet song and rest
Allures thee on from land to land.

Then fondly follow o'er the sea,
Where'er spring spreads her festival,
Guests of all climes glad wait for thee
To breathe thy blessing over all ;—

Thine own soft blessing, soft and full,
Yea, breathe upon that name once more,
That sound within itself the soul
Which consecrates each field and flower.

And far and wide o'er hill and dale,
'Mid clouds of blossom and green leaf,
Thine ancient watchword shall prevail,
Spring's faithful newly-landed chief!

Cuckoo, cuckoo! when down the host
That rallying presence first is felt—
Gliding unseen from post to post,
Winter's last ensigns turn and melt.

Yet thou no tumult dost uprouse,
Thine is no shout of victory,
Thy banners are the bursting boughs,
Thy watchword peace 'mid earth and sky.

Pilgrim, at home in every sky,
Poet, uplifting Nature's veil,
Prophet, impelled by heaven's dark eye,
Thy sacrifice of song I hail!

Ye pilgrim prophets of the Lord,
Ye poet-priests of God Most High,
Follow His voice, proclaim *that Word*,
Which broke the silence of the sky!

A MIDSUMMER EVENING IN DEVONSHIRE

Spring, the hedgerows over-topping,
From her lap no longer tosses
Woodbine clusters, richly dropping
Honey from their bugle-bosses

The lady-fern stoops o'er the shadowy spring,
In the bank fruity-red lurks the straw-streaked berry,
With new silver lined is the swallow's young wing,
And glossy the cheek of the ripe wild cherry.

The arrowy dragon-fly's black-blue gleam
With shady glance starts the slippery minnows.
What fields gold afloat as in childhood's dream !
What wealth of perfume the faint air winnows !

(A sheaf of blossom I'll lay at *her* feet !)
With milky mouths couch the young drowsy beeves,
And cows calmly plash in the old mill-leat,
'Mid the cool green light of the summer leaves.

And the ripening orange meadow-grass
Waves unbroken depths of flowers ;
And oats unripe hang their tremulous lace
In delicate pearl-green showers.

Where soft blue hills sweep grandly from the sky,
In hazy valleys float green clouds of oak :
Rippling in watery tremor restlessly
The mazy mirage breathes its silky smoke.

This soil the patriarchal ox-team broke—
Wild chant monotonous, and uncouth share !
Huge wrinkled necks bowed sullen 'neath the yoke,
Proud curving horns that idly reap the air !

The barley's long fringes and seething wheat
Spread a harvest of hope on earth's red floor ;
From the orchard alley's cool green retreat
One thrush stirs the heart of the twilight hour.

The clamorous rooks like a nation uprise,
And their black wings gleaming shiver,
Like a dark mirage in the twilight skies
They hover with dazzling quiver.

A moment marshalled, the host sweeps by
Like a darkening current of air,
Home to their towns in the elm trees high---
Like the night they settle there.

THE WHITE OWL.

INTO twilight calm and deep
    Floating low,
Float upon the wings of sleep,
    Owl of snow !

Now 'tis dark enough to see,
    Sally forth,—
For the darkness is to thee
    Starry mirth.

Stream and meadow dewy gray
    Patient course,
Flinging down upon thy prey
    With soft force !

As the voice within a dream
   Speaks unheard,
Spirit-like thy motions seem,
   Twilight bird.

Down the drowsy silence blow
   Tremulously
Hoot and wildly mellow crow !—
   Solemn glee.

So the hearts that may not sleep
   Save in light,
With the stars bright watches keep
   Through the night.

There's no loneliness on earth :
   Silence reigns
But when worlds of brighter birth
   Near our plains.

Though the light of life grow dim
   Shadowed far,
Twilight trembling round the rim
Wakes thy spiritual hymn,
   Evening Star !

THE THISTLE.

God's curse, how beautiful !
    Right regal this pink purple boss,
Though set in thorns, yet soft as moss—
    A crown and cushion cool,
Where clings the wild bee, probing far,
All velvet black with honey-bar,—
    God's curse, how bountiful !

O bee, suck honey from the curse !
  O cross, thou ladder to the crown,
O wound, that heals by making worse,
  Death dug the steps that brought heaven down !
O curse, O cure ; O cross, sweet load !
To live is Christ, to die is—God !
    Hail blessed curse of sweat, thou costly oil
    Crowning with consecration every toil !

THE KINGFISHER.

Leaving little snow-satchels o'er-brimming with scent,
Closely covered in leaves like a veiled sacrament,—
Past the hedges I hurried, and violet beds,
And wandered abroad where a stream split the meads
With its press of fresh fulness, and wild inward tone
That prevented the meadows from seeming alone.
Gold daffodils lodged in the brown broken banks
Shook their sun-lighted clusters, and thrust through
    their ranks
Paler primroses sleep in a smooth creamy crowd,
While the waterbreaks blow bubble kisses aloud.
Sheaf-like clumps of blue leaves the last snowdrop
    conceal,
Its green print in the snow stamped by fairy's fresh
    heel.
The free waters beside me with fresh liquid thrill
Now rushed forth like a river, now rippled a rill—

All its borders a tangle of roots and dry reeds,

Pebbly shoals, filtered sands, ruined stumps, and
    green weeds :

Darkly fringing its course followed bare alder trees,

That entangle in music the wings of the breeze :

And below, breaking brightly wherever I pass,

Shines a single gold crown caught in thickets of grass.

The spring was beneath me, each step of my foot

Rose elastic as pressed on some young bursting root,

And the gladness of Heaven seemed to light on the
    ground,

When I started, surprised by a quick piercing sound—
    And swift as arrow from the string,

        With one blue gleam,

        Shot down the stream

    The short kingfisher's width of wing !

    Enough, 'twas the glance of a living will

    Where all in passive joy was still,—

And how oft after anxious provisions of man

Flashes in with a silence God's unforeseen plan !

THE WOOD PIGEON.

Deep into yonder wood,
    Alone,
A bird of shyest mood
    Is flown,—

With breast of ashy blue,
    Blue-winged—
Mottled with light all through,
    Snow-ringed.

There 'mid the fir trees' gloom
    Darkening—
There in thy wild, fond home,
    Hearkening—

When all around is still,
    Earnest
Thou with whole heart in bill
    Yearnest—

Yearnest so warm and deep,
  Seeming
Like a full heart asleep,
  Dreaming.

Song leave to lightsome birds,
  Firmer,
Fuller, thine own few words
  Murmur !—

Murmur with grass and trees
  Blending,
Rest to the passing breeze
  Lending !

Wave over wave of sound
  Doubling,
Like a fount under-ground
  Bubbling.

One crush far overhead—
  'Tis gone !
Is nest so loosely laid
  Love's throne ?

SIMPLICITY.

I LIKE to see the cottage girls return
  With 'kerchiefed bundles in the eventide,
  And gaping baskets, caring not to hide
The wholesome produce of the field or churn.
Their simple independence we may learn,
  Their healthful innocence with truth allied,
  Their humble freedom where cold-hearted pride
Would make the tongue a traitor, cheeks to burn.
Shall Fashion rule our words as well as dress?
  We worship God by Fashion, and we talk
In Fashion's phrase of love and holiness!
  Up! into spirit depths take faith and walk!
Quit stagnant forms! The Christ descending stirred
The fountains of our speech—Himself the Word!

THE FIRST POPPY.

Bright Gipsy Queen of flowers,
Thou wert not nursed in bowers,
  To tumble in the breezy light
Is the joy of Summer hours !
  While there's a rugged furrow,
While there's a dusty stone,
  Right loyal for the morrow,
Thou shalt never want a throne,—
  Sure, that under God's blue dome
  Everywhere to thee is home !

Rejoice, then, to be seen,
  Thy gaiety is duty
  To Him who gave thee beauty,
Light-hearted Beggar Queen !
*   *   *   *   *
Yon barren bank's her chosen bed,
  Careless if sun or wind beat on it,
Her loose red hood thrown o'er her head—-
  My Gipsy in her scarlet bonnet !

AMBITION.

LIE silent on me, patient hand of God!
Ambition beckoning me to yonder height,
Her golden trumpet glittering in the light,
Tempts my rapt soul to scorn the lowland sod ;
She bids me wrestle from beneath Thy rod,
And rest not, till with universal sight
Snatched from the mountain's brow, in proud delight
I worship Thee where never mortal trod.

Yea, leave me not, O God! for why should I
Excel Thy creatures in pre-eminence ?
Is it not rather Satan's foul pretence
To tempt me to adore earth, sea, and sky,—
All Thou hast given to feed the outward sense,
And thus to drown Thy Spirit's inmost cry ?

AN AUGUST EVENING.

Now orange swarth the sunburnt corn o'erlies,
The butterfly spreads out its bloomy wing
Jewelled, and breathing rich transparencies ;
Fruits of all colours drink light's stainless spring.

From startled depths woodpeckers wildly laugh,
Their leaf-green plumage with gold dust o'erstrown,
With mighty bill they long to dig and quaff,
And proud head lift crown-stained with fire morone

Yon oak-stained field-floor amber stooks bestud,
Life's ancient armour piled in triumph mute—
A camping host in drowsy brotherhood,
Solemn ingathering feast of autumn fruit !

O'er upland wilds the heath, free mountaineer,
Of sinewy stem and pink of hardihood,
And golden gorse like sunshine blossoming there,
Mantle the desert with warm light from God.

Heath-purple blent with tufts of straw-pale grass
Stains the moor banks, and (crown of loneliness !)
The mountain-ash, adrip with burning mass
And weight of lustrous crimson, stoops to bless.

Bees drown their busy murmurings in your flush,
Ye rustling heather blooms ! and choked with weeds,
Trails the ribbed thorn-wreath of the bramble bush
Its glittering ebon bosses of juice beads.

The tossing poppy flaps its living flame,
Grasshoppers shake their tiny bunch of keys,
The creaking corncrake hunts its evening game,
The spider, noiseless fisher, nets aërial seas.

By leafy barn within a shadowy vale,
(Pure world of peace I never more may see !)
On fallen trunk an owl, erect and pale,
Sat motionless as statue on the tree.

It scarcely heard me, but with look serene
Slow turned and turned again its feathery poll,
Seeming the conscious spirit and the queen
Of wisdom, reigning in sweet self-control.

Too soon those snowy feathers flushed with fawn
Softly outspread, and flapping all unheard,
Beat and rebeat the valley's dewy lawn,
With countenance more human than a bird.

Low is the trickle of the summer stream,
The fiery sun has drained its silent sluice,
Spring buds it fed with liquid song and gleam,
But fruit-stained autumn finds a daintier juice.

Though seasons change, yon primitive gray tower,
Stunted, but sacred in simplicity,
Guards with its Sabbath the indwelling power,
All shadowy as the well of life should be.

How cool the ripple of the rising breeze !
Rooks wave their ragged wings in rustling flight,
The lengthening shadows of the hillside trees
Advance the stately banners of the night.

THE SUMMER TORRENT.

When clouds, black with blessing, wept heaven on
    the earth,
The whirlwind and earthquake rejoiced at thy birth,
And with shouts of deliverance kindled the strife—
Burst your gates of gray granite, ye fountains of life!
Now winds whisper vaguely where winter floods burst,
And 'mid chimings low chastened, chasms yawning
    for thirst,
Sits silence forsaken! Down furrows of wrath—
Where the torrent tore up mountain blocks in its
    path,
Where each pass was a passion, each wrench a
    ravine,
As it clove its own cliffs, and then bounded between,
Devouring, o'erwhelming, terrific and wild,—
Loose crystal threads trickle, the sport of a child!
With a child's lonely murmur, without spray or
    sprinkle,
Slips the light summer voice with its silver-like tinkle,

Down those grand rocky stairs by the Titans o'er
    thrown,
Where the thunders couch mute by each storm-
    blackened stone.
Through throngs of stone stillness stern threatening
    to leap,
Though the terror of thirst has o'erawed them to
    sleep—
Through forests of twilight where gray crags abound,
With its faint clue of light the spent rill streaks the
    ground.
For the lion whose rage winter storms but increase,
Summer leads like a lamb by the silk thread of
    peace !
Wild heart, by the red foaming thunders long riven
All tameless—how meek, like a spirit forgiven,
Thou hast bared thy rock-roots to the blue breath of
    heaven !

THE LAPWING.

THE desert's heart is thine, wild bird,
The wilderness !
There in the solitude is heard
God's tenderness.

Thy plaintive scream uplift on high,
Wilder, more free ;
My soul bounds forward with the cry,
God's liberty !

With autumn flocks seek clustering gray
The fallow downs,
With a shiver of silver breasts—away,
And darkling crowns !

A dusky vapour floats on high—
It breaks, it breathes !
Bright rippling ranks unfold and fly
In wavering wreaths.

Diving in airy circles, play
       On dark-edged wing,
O'er peaty turf now pick thy way,
       Dim, crested thing !

Then like the bird on ocean's coast,
       Feathered with foam,
Behind the moor's rock billows lost,
       Thou droppest home !

Life's borders are vast mysteries—
       Depths all unknown ;
Wings that in pride of strength uprise
       Are backward blown !

SEA GULLS.

ON SEEING FOUR SEA GULLS VERY MANY MILES INI
IN THE MONTH OF JUNE.

ARE ye sprung from ocean's feet,
Where the foamy fringes meet—
Murmuring fringe the world's wide street ?

Piercing forms all glistering white
Scarcely stain the summer light,
Wavèd wings stream wild in flight !

Steering on with steadfast eye,
Travel through the trackless sky,
Following faith's free faculty!

Sail ye high o'er earth to save
Foam-flowers cropt from some tall wave
Fresh to strew a playmate's grave?

Do ye bear on spotless wings
Peace from ocean's struggling springs?
Pearls for bridal offerings?

Mighty speed on wings of foam,
Ranging ye shall never roam,
Earth at least is not your home!

Like the breath of better lands,
Like the help of higher hands,
Like the light of blessed bands,
Ye are come and gone—
Out of silence into silence back again for ever flown!

THE WOOD SORREL.

THERE is a bank (I love it well)
Where climbs the sorrel of the wood,
Here breathes, how frail! a puce-veined bell,
There snowy droops its crumpled hood.
With knotted roots of tinctured strings
A tender tapestry it weaves,
Whilst folding back like soft green wings,
The lappets of its cloven leaves.
It is a dainty sight, I ween,
Of hoods, and bells, and fairy green ;
But when the dews of evening fall,
They mutely bless the Lord of all,
And closing, wait the daylight's call !
Hard by, o'ershadowed by the forest trees,
Like partial snow showers, wood anemones
Outstretched in level masses of white shade
People with magic companies the glade,
As flying fairy-land borne on the breeze
Had lighted round gnarled oaks of centuries,
While Spring repairs her roofless palaces.

THE RAINBOW IN THE HILLS.

ALONE among the hills, mysterious, mute,
And moveless that long sultry afternoon,
The broad suspension shadows grandly swung
From peak to peak sublimely motionless !
When lo, the cloud that seemed to quench the sun,
Spelt out upon the plain God's covenant span,
Nature's sweet silent sacrament of praise,
In lines of living colours warm as breath !
I called it (for my heart flew forth in joy)
Garland of liquid blossom dripping gems,
Heaven's arch of triumph ribbed with royal dyes,
God's battle-bow hung peaceful in the heavens !
I felt the Godhead move behind the cloud,
That self-same Voice that to the patriarch spake,
God, who, lest blindness lead man to despair,
Sudden unfolds His very garments' hem—
Untwists a wreath of light to testify
In sevenfold silence.   Many gorgeous gifts
Into one common mercy fold themselves.

13—2

Ye showers that bare the glowing veins of light,
And win its sacred secret from the storm,
Draw out anew that ancient bond of life
Which God in mercy hid within your folds!
Up! clasp, O Earth, and so complete Heaven's span,
Christ's tears have sealed the covenant *for* man!

THE WILD ROSE.

HAPPY wild rose
In the summer light born!
Fling abroad thy pink breast,
All aglow like the west,
Loosely flaked with warm snows—
Breathing breath like the morn.

Blossom of the brier,
Innocence run wild,
Clambering higher, higher,
Thrust into the light of heaven
That sweet face forgiven, forgiven,
Like a cottage child!
Wilt thou never, never tire,
Climbing, stooping, all beseech—
Be thou reconciled!

Beauty's silence moves like speech,
Spread forgiveness all may reach,
    Every cottage child !
Man cast out from Eden's bowers,
Still may gather Eden's flowers :
Even the brier runs o'er with blessing,
And the curse goes forth caressing.
Hooked with claws, and fanged with stings,
Wounds are safer far than wings ;
Cling, O thorns, and crown the strife,
First to climb the Tree of Life !

———✧✦ - ·

THE GLOWWORM.

A COMMON worm ! and yet thou wear'st more light
Than many a star deep hidden in the night !
Who, kindling, keeps thy soft green-golden lamp
Bright and untarnished 'mid earth's dewy damp ?
Or, when the dews down-dripping from the stars
Unveil night's caverned depths of glittering spars,
Did they let fall upon this bank so dark
Thy living jewel, Heaven's own vital spark ?
Day searching for a worm found what it sought,
At best a beetle, as it blindly thought ;

But night, which sees beyond this cloudy bar,
Stooped fondly o'er thee, and beheld a star !
O living fire which lights but never burns,
Gliding and glowing through the unscathed ferns,
By day a beetle, and by night a star,
I know, I feel, I recognise afar
Thy dim-discovered truth, what mortals are !—
Men saw me in the light and called me man,
But darkness quenched me, and my life began :
The immortal spirit in me shone revealed,
God's face uncovered, as earth's grew concealed.
O star-worm, spirit-light shall ne'er destroy
This common flesh I played in as a boy,
But linked together light and limb shall dwell,
And twain become one bright Emmanuel !

THE TIGER MOTH.

Float in the shadow of night !
Orange thy wings and rich parded,
Figured and blotted with velvet—
Thickening the dusk with thy stillness,
Fold thy soft plumes like a blossom !

Hooded thine head with fur helmet,
Antlered with fiercely pale feelers,
Sensitive, set with saw edges,
Float in the shadow of night—
God through the darkness beholds thee,
Fleeced with farina of flowers,
Mealy with dust of the rainbow!

Shine then my soul in night's bosom,
Hid in the dark of this human,
Eye may not see thee, but round thee
Lives the transparence of heaven.
Fixed with full face on the God-light,
Shadows and fears drop behind thee!
Darkness is God stooping o'er thee,
Sifting thy sources of being;
Darkness is God looking down thee,
Draining all light by His presence;
Darkness is but thine own shadow,
Cast by the glory above thee!

THE AUTUMN BRAMBLE LEAF.

A crimson leaf,—a leaf all blood and gold,
With its long purple stem of bramble thorns
Trailing its armèd wreath, what joy it brings
To hearts that beauty blesses with her joy !
It were the pennon of some fairy bark,
Had not a deeper impress mellowed it.
Ah ! here is autumn's own warm crimsoning,
And death lies hid beneath this leaf of gold—
Orange and crimson, violet and green—
As Autumn had drawn forth amidst decay
Even from the bramble-wreath God's rainbow sign !

It shows me though no blossoms I put forth
For men to covet, though no fruit I bear
Which fellow men will care to make their own,
Yet Heaven's own ripening dyes may stain my leaves
Ingraining glory with my helplessness—

The glory deepening as my strength declines.
So shall men say of me in pensive hope,
" And doth decay such heavenly tokens wear,
When one so lowly blendeth with the light."

NOVEMBER FOG IN THE COUNTRY.

LONG couched in slumberous folds about the hills,
Forth from its stealthy ambush now at last
Gropes up the south a mist of ashy blindness,
Drawing a humid twilight o'er the noon.
The woods are rolled in vapour, every tree
Stands mutely swathed in a blank steamy stillness ;
Slow heaving eddies huddle in the vale ;
And o'er the near and long-familiar landscape
Gray solitudes descend mysteriously !
Beneath the dense green gloom of brooding firs,
That haunt the glen with shadowy romance,
Forests of faded ferns' rich cedary stems,—
With branching plumes like fine carved cedar work,
Lie tossed and wild, where, startled by my step,
The red deer had just bounded from his lair.
Dusk larch spires wildly loom,—their short bright fur
Loose shed in saffron shadows down the slope.

The noiseless squirrel swings from tree to tree,
At home 'mid worlds of undiscovered boughs.
Driftings of purple leaves high ridge the brook,
Whose twisted stream purls o'er its matted bed.
Here scarlet hips, and darkly crimson haws,
And wreathèd strings of orange bryony
Trailed in festoons, relieve the sullen banks—
Dulled with the clammy dew, a touch dissolves
The filmy gauze, and lets them glow again.
Burning beneath a heap of rotting leaves,
The last bright chestnut's veined mahogany
Has burst its case with creamy cotton lined.
Quitting the glen which closes after me,
The floating mystery deludes my steps ;
As I approach, it visibly recedes,
I turn, it follows noiseless in pursuit.
A dreamy distance shrouds the near horizon ;
Faint muffled airs creep curdling up the midst,
But soon are lost, choked in the dewy dimness ;
Earth like a waste lies drowned in cloudy torpor,
Vague shores unknown shift strangely round
            doors.
When, lo ! the west sends streaming o'er the hill
Grand sacrificial flames of yellow cloud,
That seem to break the silence with no sound !

THE ROBIN REDBREAST.

Thy bosom is thy shield,
  Thou little robin gay,
By thy prattle and thy pranks,
By thy slim and sloping shanks,
By thy perk and nod and thanks,
Thou hast routed many a field,
  Ay, perhaps this very day.

By the twinkle of those eyes
  All a-glitter, yet so jetty,
As askance with arch surprise
  Thou wert coaxing something pretty—
Pensive silence thou canst part
  From its native loneliness,
Ever feeling round man's heart
  With a human tenderness !

Come forward to be seen,
  My little bright-eyed fellow,
(And an honest one as well O,)
  In thy suit of olive green,
  With red-orange vest between,
And small touching voice most mellow !
  Robin, all men welcome thee—
  Home's sweet heart of liberty !

WILD PRIMROSES IN DECEMBER.

ON SEEING THE WILD PRIMROSES BEGIN TO BLOOM
AGAIN ON THE FIRST OF DECEMBER.

WHAT joy when first 'mid withered leaves
  Pale lids of light unfold,
Bright buds beneath the bank's moss eaves
  Wake innocently bold !

What joy to stir around their roots
  The fragrance of fresh earth—
The crumbling dust of fallen fruits,
  And flowers of future birth !

Whose hand has stained with secret skill
  Like mellow eve each cup?
Virtue goes forth when all is still,
  And, lo! light is sprung up.

How delicate their early breath,
  When, like a silent grace,
Pink downy stalks pushed from beneath
  Breathe smiling in my face!

Again mute messages ye bear
  From One just out of sight—
From Him who rules the rolling year
  The first faint clue of light.

Ye living intercourse maintain
  With Him whose power could pause
Amid creating worlds and deign
  To give the primrose laws!

Shine, 'mid the roar of winter's storms,
  Frail fearless witnesses
Of God, whose heart conceived your forms,
  And sent you forth to bless!

Faint hearts to slender hopes must cling,
    In hope is present strength ;
To catch the first faint gleam of spring
    Makes winter half its length.

Seek the first gleam, so speed the spring,
    Not only wait but watch !
Pray at the door of hope, and sing—
    Faith's finger on the latch !

A DECEMBER EVENING.

ALL day the tempest roared from tree to tree,
Their lofty limbs shook thunders visibly !
Can leavening light crumble this vapour wall,
Or eve with golden wedge force up the dripping pall ?
At length from clouds bursts forth the living sun,
In-gushing daylight saw the day was done.
All heaven fell open naked to the eye
Sudden as when the prophet's prayer unveiled,
Amid the natural silence of the sky,
Chariots of fire and horses fiery mailed,—
Such golden glories throng the sapphire sea,
When light lets down the home of Deity.

With ruby flashes trembles the dim spire,
Red throbs the forest's restless heart of fire,
That burning up the boughs, go where you will,
Follows unmoved and flames upon you still—
Broad dazzling disc that seems to sink to rest
With quivering blaze within its woodland nest !
Fragments of rosy rainbows, crimsoned clouds,
Flush the bare trees that gathered in dark crowds
Uplift their antlered heads to breath on high,—
Dark fringed and soft as lashes veil the eye
They net the liquid primrose of the sky—
The pensive primrose melting from their grasp,
Eve's primrose peace they strive in vain to clasp.
Meek, mellowing presence hail ! mysterious rest
Lodged at the loud world's heart long unconfest !

Yon level pine groves, panelled with the light
That glows behind, transfigured on the height,
Seem fairy palaces far-stretched sublime,
Listening in awe the world's last sunset chime,
In lengthening vistas down the shores of Time !
The vision fades, and from the dreamy glen,
Haunting alone their ancient forest halls,
The dusky owls come forth from sleep to reign ;
The hollow night prolongs their echoing calls !

THE DAISY.

Thou art a ladder into Heaven,
    Small flower !
To heaven's blue heart thy silvery flashes,
That eye of gold, those snowy lashes,
Break the life-news from winter's ashes,—
    Strong tower,
Whence humblest hopes cannot be driven !

    But can I trust—
    Why art thou strong ?
    Death laid thee low
    Beneath the snow,
    But dews ere long
Drew thy young spirit back from dust.

Awake, O Earth !
The dew of Heaven
Shall all things leaven
With its new birth !
Rejoice, O Heaven !
Man's heart must first
Break, parched with thirst,
Ere God pour in—" Rise, be forgiven !"

From thy little snowy frill
Taking heaps of coinèd gold,
With a hearty right goodwill,
In thy innocency bold,
Thou dost offer back to God
All unasked thy precious load,—
Opening wide in heaven's blue face
Fingers dews had clasped in grace.

Little pillar of God's throne,
Standing forth erect and bold,
As thyself thou couldst alone
Heaven's great Majesty uphold !
On thee truly Heaven depends,
For He made thee for His ends.

'Tis pleasant, though a task not easy,
To hang one's harp upon a daisy :
Our human grasp is far too small
To feel minutely after all ;
'Tis only God can hang His power
Upon the weakness of a flower !

Lest man, grown dazzled straining at the sun,
Should find Him not, and doubt what He had done
God, stooping, wrote upon the ground in daisies,
That all who hear not should behold His praises !
This common flower men's feet tread down
His fingers wrought who wears Heaven's crown ;
And so the Flower of God was given
To be man's stepping-stone to Heaven !

THE RIVER LLUGWY, NORTH WALES.

FROM ITS RISE IN THE PASS OF NANT FRANCON TO
THE SWALLOW FALLS, BETTWS-Y-COED.

I.

BEFORE Nant Francon's awful gate,
Mid mountains stern and desolate,
Lake Ogwen darkly lies in wait,
 O'erspread with treacherous gloom.

And out of sight, though at her side,
Within huge strongholds fortified,
Llyn Idwal pours her sunless tide
 Upon a voiceless shore,

Girdled with precipices, where
Lone Echo, startled from her lair,
Bounds backward by some inward stair,
 Retreating audibly;

And from the mountain's hollow heart
Strange supernatural voices start,
As if some other world took part
    In mortal's vagrant lot !

There towering Tryfan's wedgelike form,
Whose fierce crest gleaming scents the storm,
Hastes his dark compeers to inform—
    While prattling at their feet,

Like some bright nursling strayed from home,
Yet all unconscious how to roam,
Flushed with first innocence of foam,
    Bright Llugwy quits their side—

And through the opening moorland plain,
Now scorched with autumn's russet stain,
And dashed with flying skirts of rain,
    And rainbows fading there,

She trips along with careless feet,
Delighted with her shining street,
And gleefully runs forth to greet
    Each frowning boulder block,

And fallen crag, rude sculptured o'er
With antient time's dark mystic lore,
While crystal kisses wild implore
    The unrelenting rock.

But love has her revenge, for, lo,
As day by day the waters flow,
Soft lips whose kisses melt like snow
    Have graved their image there.

And though no sound the desert stir,
Nature's own voice comes back to her,
" Love is her own biographer,
    And writes in deeds her life !"

How healing this primeval waste !
The racing river brings no haste,
The travelling heavens have not effaced
    Time's spirit brooding here.

Strange that dumb crags and melting sky,
That never knew mortality,
Should heal the spirit through the eye,
    And bathe the soul in bliss.

Here all is still, vast, changeless, free !
Heaven stoops in cloud, earth climbs to see ;
The language of eternity
　　Alone is spoken here !

Stern, rugged, background of the world,
Creation's canvas left half furled,
Dashed with celestial pictures hurled
　　By every flying gleam,—

Glorious vicissitudes are thine,
Wild heights and depths, romance divine !
Dumb souls that drink thy subtle wine
　　Brim over with new song.

II.

Climb this bold headland ; all is drear,
Few incidents of Time are here—
A wild sheep bursts the bracken near,
　　A wheeling kite shoots by ;

No harvests wave their gold, instead
Harvests of bracken, saffron red,
These frowning precipices shed,
　　Mid heather's purple gloom.

Here Time was born—from this high verge
Of nothingness—this rude rock surge—
Time's swaddling-clothes—what worlds emerge,
    Fair worlds of leafy light !

Creation's dust about us lies,
Dim stretch the grey infinities,
Vast silences of vaulted skies
    Extend from verge to verge.

Black tarns in mountain angles hung,
Or high on giant shoulders slung,
Or prone upon huge summits flung,
    Bare, lidless, and alone—

With dark eyes haunt each rocky lair,
Like Heaven's recording angel there,
Still as some supernatural snare
    Set to waylay the breeze !

O'er storm-rent chasm flood and flame
Have writ indelibly their name—
Hoar centuries still pause and claim
    News from the blind abyss.

Each crag mid flying gleams and glooms
Strange personality assumes;
Light travels through a thousand rooms,
But never rests in one.

Soft wandering vapours, wreathing round,
Remove whole mountains without sound,
Till earth seems unsubstantial ground,
And Nature spirit-land !

These mountain deserts seem to be
Suburbs of immortality—
Death comes not, and Time halts to see
Eternity go by.

Wild land of mountains, lakes, and fells—
Day's bridal dawns and flushed farewells !
Whilst torrents chime enchanted bells,
Each dawn a sabbath day—

What mysteries of light and shade
Melt lingeringly from peak to glade—
Dumb melodies divinely played
To heal the scars of Time !

Fresh foaming music from the height,
White splendour of far-leaping light,
Fill Nature's temple day and night
    With worship seen and heard.

Yon mountain gable, tempest-torn,
Seamed with unconquerable scorn,
Is Nature's palette—there blithe morn
    Mixes her colours fair ;

And there, upon the obverse side,
Westward, at eve, all sanguine dyed,
How oft, while muttering heavens replied,
    Storm signals fiercely wrought !

Here touched by dawn each sullen peak
Kindles as it were going to speak ;
There dying sunset leans her cheek
    Warm on the windy fell !

And there all day the sunbeams play
Along their visionary way,
Slant misty ladders oft assay
    Bright raids on earth's green floor,—

While slipt from bursting leash of cloud
Soft-footed troops of sunbeams crowd
And sportive storm the heights, dark-browed.
    With hurrying angel feet !

Life's noblest victories are wrought
On noiseless battle-fields of thought,
Heroic stillness that ne'er fought
    Oft wears the victor's crown.

No wild bird here unmarked may fall,
No sunset stain yon mountain wall,
But God attends the funeral
    Himself in royal state.

Wild land of vision and of rest !
Midst awe-struck clouds bent o'er the west,
God buries in thy lonely breast
    The sunsets of all time !

Then softly swims into our gaze,
O'er the world's shoulder through the haze,
All luminous with soul-like praise,
    The glittering crescent moon ;

And from her shadowy train afar,
Half veiled in innocence, a star
Steps through the dusk just where we are,
    And trembles with delight ;

Till sign and symbol evermore,
Like lights along the eternal shore,
Lift wondering nature to adore
    Love, through her star-rent veil !

Such, such is life's wild incident,
Which heaven and earth, sublimely blent,
Weave in perpetual wonderment,
    To lure the wanderer's steps !

III.

Again we join the river's side,
And, led by our sweet garrulous guide,
Like souls mysteriously allied,
    Her joys and griefs we share.

Then bounding forward with new speed,
Now clasping the brown moorland mead,
Now gossiping with rock or reed,
    The deepening waters swell ;

Till, startled by a shadowing ash,
Loud in one silver scramble dash
The laughing shallows,—flash on flash,
 Fast fly their foamy heels,—

As if bright sacks of silver spilt
Mid toppling boulders, rocks atilt,
Had (thanks to some mad fairy's guilt)
 Been squandered reckless there !

Earth still is young, do all we can
To mar the gracious primal plan ;
The child lives still within the man,
 Outgrow him as we will !

Then on again with changeful chime,
And many an old-world silvery rhyme
Learnt in some other school than time,
 The river winds and laves,—

Laves one low mountain chapelry,
With its small brood of cots hard by,
And nestling pine-girt hostelry
 Beside the sheeted lake ;

Where the still heron haunts the stone,
Or, flapping his broad wings, alone
Seeks the far twilight marge o'ergrown
     With desolation hoar.

There mighty Snowdon's triple crest
O'ershadows all the vale with rest,
Sublime on his capacious breast
     Descend the glowing heavens !

And when behind those summit spires
Eve lights unheard her altar fires,
No mortal raiment then attires
     Those dim prophetic peaks—

Charged with to-morrow's prophecies,
Already pledged in dying skies—
That seem to peer with grand surmise
     Across the lap of Time !

Till gorge, and lengthening vale, and hill,
Beneath one breathless spell lie still,
And floods of purple silence fill
     With glory homeless lands ;

Last sacrament of dying light !
Vouchsafed to Nature's waning sight,
Betwixt her and the Infinite
    Unveiled, ere darkness fall !

Dread sacrament of dying light !
And thou, transfiguration height,
Alone with One just out of sight
    Bright communing apart—

How oft I've gazed, till I, like thee,
Wrapt in Heaven's glorious privacy,
Have shared thy revelations free,
    Till earth seemed half divine !

IV.

Thence reinforced by echoing streams,
The brimming river sleeps, and seems
A pictured depth of painted dreams,
    Dissolving noiselessly.

But as it sleeps the stealing flood
Bathes autumn's rich o'erhanging wood,
That skirts yon mountain solitude
    Heaved bare against the sky.

If sunken rocks' rude points offend,
High wrathful flashes arch and bend
Bright crystal knuckles without end
        Unleaping full of light !

Now sways the current soft and full
From side to side with slumbrous lull,
While muffled voices breathe a soul
        That vanquishes all sound.

But soon though boulders choke its path,
And couching masses white with wrath,
It dashes in triumphant faith
        O'er steeps and fissures rent,—

Beneath the stagnant waterwheel,
Black crusted o'er with mossy seal—
Past shoals white birch stems half reveal,
        Adrip with leafy gold ;

Past sky-blue pool and pebbly floor,
Low grassy inlets azured o'er
(For lowliest duties by Heaven's door
        Lead unsuspecting feet);

Past the fair confluence of rills,
By silver gashes in the hills
Descending with young life that thrills
 With energy and hope,—

Till one bright moment comforted,
Then—where athwart the river's bed
A bridge, flung o'er the chasm's head,
 At one bound spans the flood,—

With bated breath, but without pause,
Hurled foaming down precipitous jaws,
One ghostly agony o'erawes
 Dumb Nature's shuddering depths,—

Anthem and agony in one
For ever pealing forth alone—
Such noble dying hath undone
 The antient shame of death.

Then quickly smoothing strife away,
As if such warfare were but play,
She smiling greets the onward way
 With snatches of bright song.

Sing on, brave singer, wildly free,
The world has need of melody,
Such notes of immortality
    Make musical dead lives !

Born in the mountains, thy pure life,
Breezy with melody and strife,
Long thrilled those dauntless precincts rife
    With mystery unsung—

But tumult deeper stillness brought,
Like pensive souls that bury thought
In soundless depths within them wrought
    By storm or sudden shock.

Sing on, wild heart ! let suffering bring
To music her last, subtlest string—
The voice of every voiceless thing
    Finds utterance in thee !

V.

Then gliding on with inward smiles,
Here cloistered within leafy aisles,
There bright unfolding lustrous miles
    Of liquid beauty's store—

The mellowing river winds and swells,
But nothing of its doom foretells,
Still murmuring broken syllables
    Of benison o'er all,—

When—with one plunge as all had died,
There sprang, triumphant from my side,
A wondrous spirit glorified,
    White thundering down the gulf!—

And instantly from Heaven's full height,
Noon's mighty archer, angel bright,
Shot dazzling shafts of glistering light,
    That smote the maddening foam—

Flashed glory through earth's brokenness,
And swift o'er her sublime distress
Flung radiant folds of righteousness,
    That clothed the black abyss

In spotless robes of paradise, that rolled
And shook tumultuous lustre from each fold,
Shechinah-glory, blinding as of old
    When seraphs veiled adored,—

Far-shining robes of spotless paradise,
Rock-shattered ever fresh before mine eyes,
Mid dazzling glory streaming from the skies,
      And loud hosannas' roar,—

When lo ! mid whirling spray and smoke,
Serene o'er all a rainbow broke—
Heaven's phantom guest, that hovering woke
      Flushed image in the foam ;

As if o'er Life's blind agony
Hope waved aloft her glorious key—
The key of Time's long mystery,
      Which Death alone reveals !

*   *   *   *   *   *

There, by the highway, ceaseless rise
Those thunders of lone sacrifice,—
Alone, mid troops of wondering eyes,
      Break, break, white Victor Soul !

THE MOUNTAIN HAREBELL.

Poets long have had their fancies,
    Sounding forth in praises loud
Each some favourite woodland blossom
    They have singled from the crowd.

But all poets here I challenge—
    (He shall dictate terms who wills !)
What so fearless—none so peerless—
    As the Bluebell of the hills !

Hail ! thou sweet blue mountain harebell,
    Delicately poised and hung,
Like the belfry of the fairies,
    By the passing breezes rung.

Hail ! bright hosts of blue pavilions
    Gaily camping o'er the ground—
Squadrons wheeling, banners flying
    At the least breath—yet no sound !

Bright blue page in Nature's volume,
  By the laughing breezes blown
Open, at some secret signal
  From a Hand upon the Throne.

Daintiest of blue umbrellas
  Wildest fairy in her fun
Ever draggled in the dewdrops,
  Ever flaunted in the sun !

Whether in the early morning
  Silvered o'er with sober dews,
Or when earth's great sunset silence
  Flushes thee with heavenly news :—

Ever with blue satchels laden,
  O'er green earth, a pilgrim band,
Ye stream forth to light the moorlands,
  Heaven-inlaying all the land.

Yes, thou art to me a passion,
  And thy silence full of song—
Scattering pure drops of heaven
  All the desert wastes along.

Threading loneliest tracts of heather
 Singly or in azure bands,
As afar mid roar of cities
 Heavenly lives link trembling hands.

Ah, the quietude of being
 Simply in thy place and sphere
Is to Him who weigheth all things
 Worship, and sublimest fear !

Trembling o'er the blackened chasm,
 Where the torrent roars all day,
Rocked mid flying foam and thunder,
 Fed with finest of the spray.—

Or where plovers wildly mewing
 Ceaseless dive in airy chase,
And quick watersparks are glancing,
 Dancing, o'er the river's face,—

There where buried murmurs deepen
 Silence, and like muffled showers,
Throngs of liquid feet are bursting
 Sweet embarrassments of flowers,—

There, midstream, thy blue smile crowneth
  Yonder storm-hurled boulder block,
Though white fairy foam-heels flashing,
  Crystal-starred, resent the shock !

Spirit of the lonely mountains,
  Spirit of the voiceless moors,
O thou frailest of God's creatures,
  Sleeping all night out of doors !

Oft alone on misty moorlands,
  Lured by thy cerulean spell,
I have watched descending twilight
  Hush with dews each chiming bell.

Whether on the heights I greet thee,
  Or by lowly fountain's brink,
I can never, never meet thee,
  But I fain would stop and think.

For thou art to me the spirit
  Of the grand heroic time,
When on Highland wastes and mountains
  Men for Truth's sake died sublime.

And thy family traditions
  Are the glowing gates of God,
Breaking wide with mystic splendour
  Round the lonely martyr's sod !

And thy family escutcheon
  Lights the deathless halls of Faith—
Poverty and Independence—
  Quartered with—Love unto Death !

For though earthly eyes see only
  Wiry stem, and steeped in dew,
Hooded face of wistful wonder
  Peering innocently through—

To me thy spontaneous beauty,
  Springing eager from the sod,
Brings to mind like distant music
  Glorious memories of God !

And though Nature call thee scentless,
  Round thee like a girdle true
I detect a deathless perfume,
  Hid in Heaven's own cloudless blue !

So however long I linger,
　Gaze upon thee as I will,
There is something left unspoken,
　And thy beauty haunts me still.

Here below mid bramble thickets,
　Where white morning mist still breathes,
Large blue dewy crowns entangled
　Meekly gleam through armèd wreaths.

There mid showers of mountain grasses
　On yon ragged boundary wall,
Like a wave of faint blue laughter,
　Bells and breezes rise and fall.

Further still, mid those same grasses
　Tiptoe on this selfsame wall,
Skyey groups are deftly playing
　Daintiest blue cup and ball !

Higher yet, betwixt dark boulders
　Where the torrent makes a gap,
One alone has climbed in sunshine,
　Tossing high one faint blue cap !

Oh, how often dashed with raindrops,
  Dauntless sapphire gem of flowers,
Over rock, and moor, and mountain
  I have followed thee for hours.

And when slowly wending homeward
  Weary down the village street,
As the old Church clock was striking,
  Lo, once more thy form I greet—

Clinging to the dusty coping,
  Half-way up the grey Church tower,
Summer after summer coming
  Like an angel to her bower !

There the swallows stoop to kiss thee,
  Wheeling in their joyous flight ;
While the dewdrops still are on thee,
  Ere the morning yet is light.

Lean awhile o'er this low gateway—
  In this plot God's seed, once cast,
Heeds nor dew, nor rain, nor sunshine,
  Ne'er comes up—till Trumpet's blast.

Yet in this lone mountain Churchyard,
  Softly o'er each grassy bed
Sky-blue tears of hope thou droppest
  Pensive o'er the sleeping dead !

Everywhere thou art a blessing
  Planted by an unseen Hand ;—
Heaven's own Resurrection banner
  Waving joyous o'er the land !

CLOUD ARMIES AND THEIR VOICES.

Clouds are divided into three classes : (1) The lower, or Rain-cloud (nimbus). (2) The central (cumulus). (3) The upper (cirrus).

HEAVEN'S three cloud-ranges, rising in their state,
Faith's slow ascending scale may illustrate.
Faith has three stations as she climbs Heaven's
  steep,
Three stages in divine discipleship—
And Faith's three peaks, each peering o'er the past,
Salvation first, then Service, HIMSELF last,—

These, like Heaven's cloud-tiers climbing layer on
    layer
Suffused with glory, form but one grand stair
Into the glorious Presence of the King,
Who covers all with His o'ershadowing Wing !
For though rank differ both in cloud and saint,
Round all alike the same blue Heaven is bent.

Ye Rain-clouds first, too swift to overflow
With penitential tears where'er ye go—
Restless and dark and rent as from within,
And tempest-driven as with ghosts of sin,
Dragging your weeping wings along the ground
That might have cleaved God's heavens with rainbow
    bound !—
Your fruitful showers that first fed famished earth,
Their own fair fruits too often drown at birth,
Forming and falling, falling evermore,
Till harvest gold lies rusting on Earth's floor !
What though Earth ne'er her fruitfulness could show
If darkening showers are wanting,—yea, what though
Contrition's tears, like childhood's, must have place,
Must childhood's tears then *always* soil the face ?
Must sorrow's showers alone no light betray,
'Though smit by sunset's penitential ray ?

And cleansing tears, unlike God's sunlit rains,
Unravel no fair rainbow's glowing skeins
Of liquid light and lustre o'er Earth's stains ?
If hope from Heaven point out the shining track
Must storms of guilt for ever beat man back ?
The Past so hold our vision, that at last
We live no Present, but one blotted Past ?
If Grace invite confession to detach
Souls from their sin, shall Faith not lift the latch ?
Since Calvary's sunset crimsoned Nature's skies,
The rent blue Heavens above us cloudless rise,
God lights us home with flames of sacrifice !

You next, ye shining hosts, that bask and brood
And float majestic through the solitude
And crowded stillness of Light's fairest lands,—
High linked sublime in long celestial bands
Whose soaring heights and glistering shoulders bare
Shed an immortal lustre through the air,—
Veil, veil in light your footsteps !—while unfurled
Bright stream your stainless banners o'er the world !
With upward gaze and widening wings that press
Through radiant worlds of everlastingness,
Speed, thronging Forms, all lustrous with delight,
Revealing gulfs of azure in your flight,
God-lit, yet lighting God's far infinite !

But lo, arrested by some Voice on high,
What eager wings impatient chafe the sky ?—
What sudden whisper changed your mighty course,
Wheeled your tumultuous squadrons ?   Has prayer's
     force,
As once on Carmel, yon far cloudflake driven
Like a man's hand to fill Faith's hungering heaven ?
I know not, but I know Faith longs to share
Your boundless tracts of shining service there—
With you to walk your lofty round in light,
And run the Master's errands in His sight—
Waylay His glory at morn's opening gate,
Prolong His splendours ere it closes late ;
Far into dark recesses of the soul
His Mercy's soft cloud-chariot wheels to roll ;
And spurning lofty tracts of dazzling ease,
Like you transmit His light, and grandly seize
Time's splendid opportunity of tears
For angel ministries between the spheres,
And thus fulfil the soundless march of years !

You last, ye spirit-clouds, all ranges past,
Least seen, most sainted, first and therefore last !—
Who from your own far white eternity
Seem gazing on into some holier sky—

O ye that, pure, and still, and higher yet,
Light wreathed about the Sovereign Master's feet,
Still bear your silent witness evermore,
Nor witness less, because ye worship more!
Not lustrous now, stript bare of glory's dress,
Self-stript, for lo! frail white unworthiness,
And voiceless adoration's awful love,
And your own nothingness His nearness prove!
Not lustrous now, too near His face to shine,
But feeding on that wondrous Face Divine
In unveiled vision, still, oh still, maintain,
High o'er this struggling earth, ah, not in vain,
Your stainless Sabbath—for to gaze is gain!
Ah, not in vain your virgin fleece is spread
Before His feet, to tempt the Master's tread;
Not vain, white poised, on victor wings ye lie
Arrested, held by Heaven's near harmony;
Content beneath those wounded feet to be,
The spotless dust of passing Deity!
Ah, not in vain outstretched in spent repose,
Ye ever linger, lost in love that knows
No limit of intensity or time,
Voiceless, absorbed, insatiable, sublime—
High pledge serene of man's seraphic goal,
Sabbath of rest that waits each struggling soul!

The paved work of a sapphire stone in sight,
Each breathing vein transparent with pure light,
Thus to be nothing, lost to all estate,
Save just to let the Life-blue penetrate
Your every fibre with life not its own,
Then breathe it stainless back before the Throne !
With tenderness alone the contrite share,
And something of seraphic shyness there,
Yours the new dawn, when storm-clouds break and
      pass
And timid rays fresh woo the tangled grass—
Virtues and victories laid proudly down,
To crown His feet is Love's supreme life-crown !
Then gaze yourselves away from day to day,
The wondering guests of immortality !
High o'er earth's restless currents' ebb and flow,
Awed by His nearness whom 'tis life to know,
His Presence, nay, HIMSELF, so fills all gaze,
None minister, none worship, and none praise !

LONDON.

All-sovereign City, glorious in thy state,
  Imperial in thy daring, boundless, free ;
  Thou central wheel of time, yet like the sea
Forlorn, unfathomable, desolate—
Gathering all nations through thy open gate,
  And pouring forth thy miser wealth with glee,
  Yet shuddering with thy dens of poverty,
And gathering blackness daily, guilt, and fate !
Who shall deliver thee ? who dost thyself
  Deliver all men, reckless of the cost ;
  Scenting all haunts of slavery thy boast—
Yet harbouring at thy heart, for damning pelf,
Hell's demon workshops grinding under breath,
With one lone exit at the rear, called—Death !

PATERNOSTER ROW.

Under the shadow of St. Paul's proud dome,
  Heaving its huge blanched shoulder high in air,
  For generations unmolested there,
The rooks of literature have built their home.
From the four winds of heaven they come, they come,
      come,
  Mid infinite tumult wondrous stores they bear,
  Darkening with pendent nests Fame's thorough-
      fare,
While clouds of issuing broods launch forth to roam.

Strange roving colonists are these skilled rooks,
  Sowing light's mystic seed in every land,
Wafting life-blood of souls embalmed in books,
  Binding earth's death-wounds with Truth's spell-
      writ band—
Their field the world!—Shade of St. Paul, still
      foster
These winged soul-powers, till time's last Pater
      noster!

ON RECEIVING BACK SOME REJECTED MSS.

Welcome, sweet children, to your home again,
  And did blind publishers not see your worth,
  Never suspect your high immortal birth?
And when thrust scared into vile city den,
Those innocent faces, did they plead in vain?
    Then hear me, bright babes, strains now bad men's
        mirth,
    Their dainty dialect too pure for earth,
Shall be posterity's proud priceless gain!

Long welcomed, recognised, and wooed in heaven,
  Flash, angel guests, but once through bars of
        print,
And your coarse judges blinded, unforgiven,
  Shall perish without further hope or hint!
Genius alone can genius recognise,
None else detect immortals in disguise!

ST. PAUL'S FROM LUDGATE HILL.

A SOLEMN awe o'erwhelms me at the sight
Of yon huge Temple (thro' whose smoke-wove
    shroud
Outworn at angles breaks a weird grey light)
Uplifted head and shoulders o'er the crowd
Of endless habitations,—like a cloud
Hung brooding domelike o'er the infinite
Hoarse roar beneath, where wealth and want aloud
Wrangle for treasure as in mortal fight !
Long may that shrine's colossal solitude
Upswelling vast, instinct with tidings dread
Of other worlds, its solemn bulk intrude
O'er roaring highways,—voice as from the dead
Soundless, yet heard above the multitude
Surging like sleepless torrent in its bed !

THE CROWN OF JUBILEE, 1887

THE crown of Jubilee at length is thine—
All other crowns long since fond Heaven let fall—
Fair Honour's crown in all things great and small
With Home's rose chaplet nobly didst thou twine;
Then Victory's laurels, Faith's gold wreath divine,
Clasped Purity's white blossoming coronal—
But Sympathy's star-crown outshone them all,
As godlike Love all virtues doth outshine.
Thus crowned with spoils of fifty kingly years,
By fifty peoples garlanded to-day,—
Yet that brow loves her diadem of tears,
One deathless hand still shares thy sceptre's sway !—
In the brave dark of grief's long, long arrears,
Love still grows wings that pant to fly away !

A MILITARY FUNERAL AT ST. PAUL'S.

WESTWARD the mighty portals were flung wide,
   And with death's gorgeous pageant there swept in
   Floods of rich light like wings of seraphin,
Till all the moted air shone glorified,
And from its quivering pulses' living tide
   Strange mystic fervours throbbed forth, such
      ween
   As when some strong emotion the unseen
Eternal Silence has with earth allied.

O then without, mid surging throngs to stand,
   And feel the world's great pulse with one accord
Beat for a single instant in your hand,
   And thence conjecture ever afterward
The boundless life-throb of all creaturehood
Held in the patient sheltering hand of God !

GORDON'S DEATH:

THE FIRST ANNIVERSARY IN LONDON.

IMPERIAL CITY, canopied with cloud
    And mists self-woven—heavenless half the year,
    Thyself, instead of one far friendless bier,
Art justly wrapt to-day in funeral shroud !
For he, brave man of men, child, warrior, saint,
    Great Nature's own uncoroneted peer,
    Was crowned to-day, by traitorous Arab spear,
Monarch of heroes, martyr without taint !
Lord of the lion-heart, lone guest sublime
    Of high God mid far deserts, whose least aim
    And common footstep was unconscious fame
Resounding through the corridors of time—
From land to land thou sped'st like some swift flame,
Purging all wrong—world-patriot thy name !

TURNER'S SKIES IN THE NATIONAL GALLERY.

Bold reveller in colours !—not a storm
 Of maddest passion that e'er rent the frame
Of Nature's incommunicable form
 But, captured by thee, shares thy deathless fame.
Swirls of tempestuous vapour—glorious shapes
 Of unimaginable mystery chase
Through teeming air joy's phantom that escapes,
  While worlds of undreamt wonder loom through
   space.

Such were Creation's primitive wild tones,
 When first pealed forth the echoes of that Voice
Which shook the morning stars upon their thrones,
 And bid a newborn universe rejoice!
And still the untarnished splendours of a God
Deck with undying colours Time's abode !

J. M. W. TURNER.

POET in colours, swathing every theme
   In visionary robes of glory wrought
On mystic loom, wild seer in a dream
   Whose soul burns through the symbol of his
      thought—
Thou weav'st a spell of magic sympathies
   Round seas and shores and ancient gulfs of Time—
Fair stainless cloudland's floating terraces
   And golden promontories stretched sublime.

Thine eagle glance, outpiercing mortal sight,
   Doth seize the vital moment of each hour,
And flood the very sunshine with new light,
   And flash new glory 'thwart the rainbow shower.
Breathing o'er all thy singing soul, despite
Of dying glooms—Time's rich transcendent dower.

WESTMINSTER ABBEY.

TREAD softly, stranger, every step you take
  Is paved with death—here sleep the mighty dead !
  Invisible hosts beside you soundless tread,
Inaudible choirs around soft music make ;
Echoes of immortality awake
  Hoar aisle and cloistered avenue,—and red
  Undying sunset from rich windows shed,
Like Christ's most holy Passion, for His sake
Paints the pale sleeping marble from on high
  With Heaven's pathetic mercy,—and reveals
  The mighty past, which death awhile conceals,
More awful in omniscient Memory !
Tread softly therefore, stranger ! God alone
Here guards His own crown lilies, blossom-blown.

THE PALACE OF WORDS.

WITHOUT AND WITHIN.

I stood without the gates of Westminster,
   While, crowned with clamour, England's chief
      passed by,—
And watched a flock of circling pigeons high
Wheel in white clouds of innocence mid-air,
Till soft on winnowing wing they lighted there,
   Right in the very courtyard fearlessly,
   Unheeding the proud State's imperial eye,
Or surging crowds, or April's stormy glare.

But ah ! within, the wrangling Fates, I ween,
   With soulless and irrevocable shears,
Carving what must be from what might have been,
   Scared the fair Future's white-winged flock of
      years—
Blind to a thousand beckoning hands unseen,
   Heedless of Hope's rich sun-gleams and her tears !

THE PARKS IN MAY.

Ye breeze-swept lungs of London, domed with great
  Immeasurable fields of sapphire hue—
  Heaven's own unfathomable soul-like blue—
Encamping o'er you in crystalline state !
What rest, what freedom here the desolate,
  Din-hunted wanderer finds, whose soul, still true
  To Nature's instincts, craves her healing dew
Mid this stern wilderness of human fate !

Here, in this green dell, girt by hum of men,
  'Twixt stream and verdure half sequestered still,
I've watched to-day the busiest waterhen
  Carving from belts of sword-flags with her bill
Broad leaf on leaf, then rowing shy and fast
Back with her trophy where she hid the last.

TO A SULPHUR BUTTERFLY,

FRAIL wind-tossed butterfly 'twixt city walls,
   Wavering uncertain in thy bright career,
   Like some ethereal sky-born voyager,
Heaven-launched, but 'twixt two worlds' conflicting
      calls
Bewildered as by rival festivals,
   Mortal or else immortal !   Do not fear—
   We, too, once breathed celestial atmosphere,
Man's sun-burnt limbs once ranged ambrosial halls :
For I, too, claim Divinest ancestry—
   My father ruled earth's kingdoms for his own,
   And wore Creation's jewels in his crown—
And oft at eve all Immortality
Stood crowding unabashed his sunset gates,
But *wavering* lost him all his proud estates !

17

LONDON SPARROWS AND THEIR SPRING PLANS.

A SPARROW in Spring clad in soft sable vest,
While preening his wings on the branch of a tree
At the back of a nobleman's house in the West,
Set the sparrows around him all giggling for glee.
"The lord whom I keep as my gardener," quoth he,
"(Just to get the girls' cheeks with blush-roses new
    drest)
I've sent out of town for a good fortnight's spree ;
Cousin Skylark's, in Hampshire, I thought would be
    best.
For it seemed quite a sin not to give them a run,
After toiling so hard half undrest in such heats ;
So the poor girls for once shall enjoy some pure fun,
Where they've no bones to pick, and no wrangling for
    seats.
For, of course, after Easter when Parliament meets,
Live wares must be hawked up and down through the
    streets !"

GENIUS AND COMMONPLACE.

Genius and Commonplace went forth one day
    Together from their homes to seek employ;
    Genius with his large eyes dilate with joy
Saw glory at his side in bright array
Painting immortal pictures all the way,
    Which Time soon mellowed with his rich alloy :
    But Commonplace would oft with doubts annoy—
What coloured feathers in hope's pinions, pray.

At length they reached the spot where streams divide.
    Quoth Commonplace, I'll bind me to this mill ;
But Genius with seraphic voice replied,
    I'll paint my cheeks with breezes on Fame's hill,
Dreams of immortal beauty dare my pride !
    So Genius sang, and Commonplace grinds still.

A CITY THUNDERSTORM.

The mighty city slept at brink of morn,
  When suddenly there swept athwart the sky
  Wild thunder peals, that, rolling horribly,
Fled swift as phantom courier tempest-born,
Dashed with dismay, who in his flight hath torn
  Dark seals of fate and startling prophecy—
  While from his hoofs the fiery lightnings fly,
And baleful wings of doom spread flushed with scorn
High in the very rafters of God's heaven
  Hell hangs his fiery nest and lightning brood,
Nor ever till night's tempest vault is riven,
  Doth earth half know her awful solitude—
Till hurtling wings, hot flaming, downward driven,
  Reveal black guilt by Heaven's swift sword pursued

TRUST.

STAND forth, my soul, and fling mistrust aside,
   Take God's great truth for thine and build thereon,
   Lean on that Arm invisible i' the sun,
This be thine only armour, there abide.
Trust for the future Him whom thou hast tried.
   What hast thou thou canst keep?   To Him alone
   Belongs the past, who calls it still His own;
Future and Past both hail Him Guest and Guide!
All-present Spirit!   Hail, thou dread " I Am !"
   The future stands before Thee like a sea—
   Far-stretching mirror; and the Past doth flee
Within Thy shadow, echoing back Thy name,
   Ever retreating, followed still by Thee,
Who fillest all with Thy stupendous fame!

DISTRUST.

Some souls there are, which dim the light of heaven,
   Fling darkness in God's face, however fair,
The light of joy and love which He hath given
   They mar with doubts, as only weakness dare :
   Sifting their sorrows with a keener care
Lest aught escape, at length when they are driven
   To desperate shifts, they set themselves a snare,
Then wrestle with the wrongs for which they've
   striven.

O lead them to behold pale sorrows' Chief !—
   Under whose seamless garment clung within
   The world's great woe, the seamless coat of sin —
Who, for the joy before Him, scorned relief ;
   And while fear's shadow hid what He would win,
Shut calmly on Himself the gates of grief !

TILL THE DAY DAWN.

The world is sleeping—but high, wakeful stars
  Lie strewn across the abysses of the night;
  Here in dark depths pants some deep pool of
      light,
There showers of jewels flash like scimitars !
All heaven keeps open festival, none mars
  The universal purpose of delight;
  Ten thousand gateways to the infinite
Stand beckoning, heedless of all Nature's bars.
But lo ! a paleness from the East, most faint,
  Steals over night's broad brow—what signal durst,
What dumb thing in hushed chamber durst acquaint
  With dawn's pale secret the lone sufferer first ?
  Faintly yon mirror gleams !—with such fine thirst
Love's sensitive soul waylays Christ's Dawn, rapt
      saint !

CONFIRMATION DAY.

Young feet unheard throng up Redemption's stair—
 " Defend, O Lord, Thy children kneeling now
Low in Thy temple hushed in solemn prayer,
 Seal Thou, Great God, seal Thou each struggling
 vow !"
At once from heaven in swift response, I trow,
 Aslant from latticed window high in air,
Shot noiselessly athwart each kneeling brow
 A fluted shaft of quivering sunlight fair.
Dusty, and broad, and many-ribbed it fell,
 But, as it touched each gossamer veil of snow,
Kindling into a light insufferable,
 Each buried head seemed steeped in deathless
 glow—
Let infant faith but touch prayer's secret bell,
 The God of glory deigns Himself to show !

AFTER A MISSION.

Hail, sacred tumult, strange immortal strife !
  Force matched with force, and host beleaguering
      host
  In deadly soul-siege,—earth's proud banners tost
Madly from wounded hands round springs of life !
Hail, Sinai's thunders, tears, and priestly knife,
  Woes of the self-slain, wailings of the lost !
  Hail, shouts of landing on Faith's sunlit coast,
With summer wafts of deathless music rife !
High o'er the surging throng Heaven's messenger,
  Eager and calm as from some rock-built height,
  Sways with one spirit sword celestial bright
That mighty sea of straining souls that stir
  And quiver with each flash, till o'er sin's night,
  And that vast conscience hushed, bursts glory-light !

A MODERN CONFESSOR.

Spurgeon, that pregnant mother wit of thine
  Still thrills the world to laughter and to tears—
  Tears that lure soul-wrecks past the briny years,
Laughter that makes doubt's mist-rolled icepeaks
    shine.
Thy honest tongue's a magic looking-glass
  Where lost men find themselves *themselves* once
    more,
  And rend with scorn the masks long years they
    wore,
And bless again blue heavens and green, green
    grass.

Thine is a rugged, manly, royal soul,
  Like some bold crag suffused with waterfalls,
Veiling in rainbow spray the thunder roll
  Of torrent voices and their trumpet-calls.
Thy mighty artless bow of common-sense
Drives shaftlike home God's Whither and God's
    Whence !

A WINTER'S SUNSET IN HYDE PARK.

RIGHT at the heart of the great central roar
Of Babel worse confounded than before,
I stood alone ; an ample solitude
Of green savannah lightly fringed with wood
Encompassed me on every side ; clear sky,
Deep, limitless as God's infinity,
Pressed down in silence o'er me like God's ear
Stooped low in one vast canopy to hear.
Fresh hurled in ruthless ravage, tempest-strown,
Huge limbs of ancient trees, like giants thrown
By some invisible wrestler in the night,
With mute pathetic ruins met my sight.

Beyond, on the horizon's dusky bound,
Cleft by the clasping blaze that girt them round,
Detached and solemn, stood forth each dark trunk,
Wrapt in the flaming orb, which, dazzling, sunk

Behind the matted elm-trees in the west,
Where, brooding down on his low burning nest
With quivering wings of sunset, lo, far rays,
Like angel arms flung high in mute amaze,
Shot widening up the zenith flushed with praise.

I turned, and suddenly the crescent moon,
Unearthly pure that winter's afternoon,
With her white silver sickle's finest blade
Through falling swathes of cloud a pathway made
Like some celestial reaper 'mid the grain,
Whose shining furrows quickly closed again
Grateful about her feet,—such strokes of love,
Such ghostly wounds, Heaven's healing virtue prove
I lingered long, and when I plunged at last
Back where the tide of life poured madly past,
That vision of God's peace still held me fast.

WINDSOR PARK.

MID stretches of vast woodlands flushed with May—
    A thousand oak groves and far forest bowers—
    Windsor's stupendous pile, bright dashed with
        showers,
O'ershadowing half a shire majestic lay.
No ruin there breathed mute appeal, but gray
    Impalpable mystery of romance still dowers
    That mighty coronal of glorious towers
With feudal despotism's noblest sway.
For here, encircled in this broad green realm
    Of nature's antient peace, the loftiest Soul
    In all her kingdom wields sublime control
(Her widowed hand still faithful to the helm !)
O'er her world-empire !—this her proud decree—
Nations of light, arise, link hands, be free !

ON AN ANTIENT SUN-DIAL.

Within the stately garden of the soul
   Where winding alleys meet and sheltering bowers,
   Fronting fair glimpses of immortal towers,
That from blue heights afar command the whole,—
There in mid-space, beneath high Noon's control,
   Within hushed court of verdure green with showers,
   Life's sun-dial—Conscience—guards the God-given
      hours,
Like Heaven's high envoy meting out man's goal.
Dread arbitrating angel hid in clay !
   Commanding every mortal avenue,
Bared to the light of Heaven the livelong day,
   Adjusting with swift scales true and untrue,
On wavering wills Thy sceptre proudly lay—
   No shadow indicates Heaven lost to view !

LIFE'S BATTLE.

THE men that fight the battle of the world
    Are not the indomitable wills, all health ;
    Nor are they the inheritors of wealth,
Who sit in high seats 'neath proud banners furled ;
Nor are they the keen intellects with curled
    And supercilious lips, that plan by stealth
    To steal a march on honour where she dwell'th,
From self-reared eminence soon rudely hurled.
But they are oft the passive on their beds,
    Who inch by inch fight the slow fight of life !
    And oft obscured mid masses in the strife,
Lost in the mist of numbers that o'erspreads
The city's dense heart,—pale Toil grandly weds,
    Mid tears, fair immortality to wife !

RICHMOND PARK, THE FIRST OF JUNE.

Soft billowy depths of foliage, far away
    Lost in blue skirts of dreamland, on my sight
    Burst like a vision from this terraced height,
Fresh crowned with antient sylvan peace to-day.

And through yon glorious valley toward the west
    Unfolding its fair bosom evermore
    Mid Eden bowers like Hiddekel of yore,
Soft flowing Thames inlays the land with rest.

Mid vesper glooms the muffled chestnuts stand;
    White bridal hawthorns bowed down with pe
        fume,
    Their thorny branches blunted with snow-bloom,
Breathe summer's odorous blessing o'er the land !

Gnarled pollard oak-trunks, weird, like ruined towers
  Soft islanded in bracken stand knee-deep;
  While brooding stock-doves rock the woods to
    sleep,
Redoubling drowsy murmurs from hid bowers.

And from the lighted beech-tree's topmost stair
  The thrush, unchallenged through his echoing
    hall,
  In crystal tones most urgent, musical,
Lays down the leafy laws of praise and prayer.

How noiselessly (through glimpses in the trees)
  Soft troops of fallow deer range o'er the mead,
  Lending deep rest of unexpended speed
To slumbrous old-world depths of wooded ease.

O'er many a lawny upland, dappled plain,
  Summer once more plays her old sylvan games—
  Broad oaks in shadow proudly print their names,
While laughing sunshine blots them out again.

Ye rhododendron alleys, populous
  With dusky creatures listening round their doors—
  How soundless o'er your honeycombed turf floors
They dart in gambols in and out the house!

Bright sheets of water lying in the grass
  Waylay me, as I skirt the thicket-side
  Unthinking, till, half startled, I espied
Myself outstretched in Nature's looking-glass.

With reedy marge the still lake glimmering lies—
  Pure sensitive white soul, that all unheard
  Gives back each fleeting image of the bird,
And paints the liquid landscape of the skies.

Here pause, and from this breezy eminence
  Of rippling beech-groves, watch, as zephyr stirs,
  How golden gleams like angel trespassers
Push noiseless through the leafy curtains dense.

Blue sheets of hyacinth fringe yonder fence,
  Red glides the squirrel swift from tree to tree ;
  Close coursing the sweet turf, the solemn bee
Gleans Nature's gold with dainty diligence.

Deep set in earth like windows into heaven,
  Up through the greensward, lo ! bright pools sky
    blue
  Break in like consciousness restored anew,
Or like some deeper sense to Nature given.

Now shadows lengthen round me unaware,
   The glow of sunset mellows wood and lea,
   The throstle's voice is mute upon the tree,
The hush of worship holds the enchanted air.

Bruised herbage now exhales love from the sod,
   And the soul enters realms of peace unheard—
   Unnoticed save by lonely coppice bird,
And all around me lies the grace of God.

Earth's teeming concords sound from shore to shore,
   The seraphim of Nature never fail !
   Law chimes with law till lost within the Veil,
Creation is creating evermore !

AN OLD MOUNTAIN SIGNPOST REVISITED

THAT withered arm still vigorously points
  Up towards the sleepy hollow far away,
  Hid mid the dreaming hills for time and aye,
Where dawn's first virgin kiss the crags anoints,
And eve, tired eve, strips off her amethyst—
  And the wild grace of Nature still survives
  In gentle tragedies of obscure lives,
And silent shepherds still brave storm and mist.
There shy young souls, upgrown by breezy fell,
  All colour of their years from Nature draw—
  The changing seasons their eventful law,
And grey tradition lingering haunts the dell ;
And one weird yew guards, dateless chronicler,
The meek dust of God's unforgotten there !

SYRIAN HILLS.

SACRED SONNETS.

ABRAHAM.

This word came forth to Abraham while he slept
  Beneath a mighty canopy of stars—
  " Lift up thine eyes on high !"—through Time's
    rent bars
Flash star-worlds !—footprints where a God has stept
Across the abysmal spaces—and like these
  Strong, countless, lo ! on Faith's rapt vision start
  (Lift up thine eyes, O sleeper, where thou art !)
Star-anchored fleets of sheltering promises !

But Christ, lest Heaven's high mysteries confound
  Or dark life-secrets baffle mortal sense,
Stooping, picked up Truth bloom-ripe from the
    ground,
  And lilies preach the laws of providence—
Look up ! rent heavens blaze thick with covenant
    seals,—
Look down ! wild love-blooms bless faith's bruisèd
    heels.

LOT.

— — — —

Alone at eve Lot sat in Sodom's gate,
  Revolving earth's abounding wickedness
  'Mid deep soul-tumult, when, in mortal dress
Disguised, two angels urgent entered late.
That night solved mysteries of human fate ;
  Those angel faces fair, 'mid fiendish stress
  And carnival of sin, in vain repress
The anguish of immortal anger's weight !
Scarce was night's scene of blasting blindness o'er,
  And waves of hellish laughter ebbed away,
When, ere the dawn, torn from that desperate door,
  Angel-impelled, Lot dared no longer stay.
The rest is writ in fire—God spake no more—
  Home, children, wealth, wife, honour, lost that
    day !

JACOB'S DREAM.

A FUGITIVE, self outlawed, so he fled
   All day in tumult through the rocky waste
Alone with the great silent sun o'erhead,
   Alone all day, till eve, eclipsed in haste,
Drew all her splendours after her, and shed
   A deeper solitude, when he, sin-chased,
Homeless and worn, at length upon a bed
   Of bare rock sank,—fair dreams his fears effaced.
A shining ladder, like a royal ray
   Shot from the inner Throne, stood at his feet
Trembling with light, love-thronged—an instant way
   Of escape heavenward ! Whence a Voice, soul-
      sweet,
   Woke him with transport,— twas God's mercy-
      seat !
Great stars leaned out of heaven, earth breathless lay.

BALAAM.

To will is noble, but 'tis nobler still
    Manfully to undo the will again
    Too rash resolving, warped by guile or gain—
But nought of this recked Pethor's proud seer, till
Hell-urged by his own blind sin-clenched self-will,
    Nor bursting golden honour's galling chain,
    He madly dares to ride down God in vain,
Dark trafficking with the invisible !
Ah ! spotless angel, standing in the path
    Of headlong passion, still " into the field "
Turn guilt aside from Heaven's unsheathèd wrath !
    Still, with " crushed foot against the wall," c
        shield
Impious Self-ruin riding on to death,
    Smiting dumb circumstance that dares not yield !

JOSHUA.

Dark reconnoitring now the haughty walls
 Of Jericho—doomed Canaan's towering boast,
 The heroic captain of the pilgrim host
Arrested stands—what warrior form appals ?
What light is that where darkness deepest falls ?
 Haste, Joshua, haste, stand barefoot in the dust,
 Nor angels in disguise as foes accost,—
From glooms of Jericho Emmanuel calls !
Faith abdicates her throne to crown her Lord—
 Sees grace prolonged in glory's dull delays ;
Conscience once sheathed, she fears no other sword,
 No dread Hereafter of her yesterdays,
But facing dauntless, danger, doubt or doom,
Her gates of triumph are the closing tomb.

GIDEON.

Care-blind he toiled, nor dreamed how by the oak
　Of Ophrah sat God's angel—so to-day
　God's angels meet and pass us in the way !
" The Lord is with thee," thus the angel spoke,
" Thou mighty man of valour."　Gideon woke
　From his long life-dream—" If, if so, I pray,
　Then why—where—but—it cannot be, ah, nay !"
Thus doubt's dark swarm o'er Heaven's fair vision
　　　broke.
Then on him bent the Angel his full gaze,
　As when a May sun, swift lest stealthy shower
Tarnish her blooms, unbinding her pent rays,
　Rebuke becomes transfiguration hour—
" Go thou in this thy might—give God the praise—
　By one look launched upon Almighty power !"

JEPHTHAH'S VOW.

"WEEP not, child, victory shall soon be ours,
  And sire and maid once more in peace shall dwell,
  One last kiss—victory, then home! Farewell!"
Thus bravely he strode forth 'mid citron bowers,
Palm groves and figs, where now dark battle lowers
    O'er Ammon's vales, when, hark! like clarion
        knell
    This vow rang forth—"Take, Lord Invisible,
Whate'er shall come forth first from Jephthah's
        towers,
If he return in peace, proud Ammon slain!"
    He sped, and fought, and conquered gloriously,
And soon stood victor at those gates again;
    But when that fair maid bright with jubilee,
Timbrel and dance, burst forth with virgin train,
    He childless stood, life-shattered, 'mid her glee!

ELIJAH IN THE WILDERNESS.

ALL day he fled from the revengeful queen,
  Till now nigh lost mid desert strongholds drear,
  Prostrate beneath the sun-scorched juniper,
His torn soul craves to quit this mortal scene.
Is this my lord Elijah's wonted mien,
  Whom Cherith's dried-up music cost no tear?—
  The raven's pensioner, Truth's dauntless seer,
Mysterious potentate of worlds unseen?
  Whose rugged heart to Nature's fastness clung
Whilst edges of humanity he strode,
  Dread keys of doom about his girdle hung,
Man's terror, though the trembling guest of God,
  With heaven's high secret charged?—yet now, fear
      stung,
    The lord of drought and fire flees woman's tongue

ELIJAH ON CARMEL.

One rugged form leans dark against the sky
  High upon Carmel's steep; he stands alone
  By Heaven's rude altar reared of storm-rent stone,
The famine-stricken hosts crouched wondering nigh.
Let Baal's baffled bleeding priests vain try
  To hide their shame in ribald wrath, and own
  Defeat with curses; calm his proud eye shone,
Himself God's last lone beacon set on high.
Then with gaunt hands uplift to heaven, he cried,
  " Let it be known this day Thou art the same
Jehovah Lord, Thy Name be magnified !"
  And instantly the mighty answer came,
And faith and fire for ever were allied,
  And the stern Prophet's marble brow glowed flame

ELISHA.

Smitten with blindness, so he led them on,
  (Heaven's bodyguard of fire still o'er him bent,
  Though veiled in morn's translucent firmament !)
Till now the baffled hosts, surprised, undone,
Within Samaria's armèd heart alone
    Stand, sightless captives doomed,—when lo, prayer
      rent,
    Heaven flashed back new sight, and, strange sacra
      ment !—
Foe feasts with foe while mercy's sun outshone.
  Thus, ye processions of dim sightless souls,
Led in divine arrest by ghostly seer,
  Captives of Calvary, ye whom thunder-rolls
Chase to the far brink of sublime despair—
  The immeasurable dark of utmost heaven
  By one stupendous flash of Mercy's riven !

THE QUEEN OF SHEBA.

O FAIR she stood, far Sheba's dauntless Queen,
    With mighty train, and camels stored with spice,
    Gold, precious gums, and gems beyond all price—
'Mid Salem's dazzling towers she stood serene,
Her eyes starlit, foreign her garb and mien—
    But who shall paint her twilight soul's surprise
    As the King's speechless splendours met her eyes
His deathless lore unveiled things seen, unseen !
    " It was a true report I heard, O King,
In mine own land, but I believed it not,
    Such glory passeth earth's imagining !"
So, life's long journey o'er—lo ! without spot
    New-landed innocence, bliss-crowned, shall stand,-
    " It was a true report I heard in mine own land !"

ISAIAH.

THAT year the King died—I, disconsolate,
　Struck dumb by Heaven's inscrutable dark skies,
Stood worshipping within the temple gate,
　Soul-rapt, at hour of evening sacrifice,
　When, lo ! the Veil rent, and before mine eyes
God's orbèd Majesty enthronèd sate,
　All veiled about with awful sanctities,
While quivering thresholds moved with glory's weight !
Oh, then these ears throbbed with the beat of wings,
　These burnt lips glowed with strange unearthly fire,
Man's eyes drank visions of the King of kings,
　Half lost in light, half blinded with desire !
　At last a Voice spake, like some long-lost lyre
Love-struck, new soul leapt down life's wondering
　　strings !

BELSHAZZAR.

THE Queen within her chamber sat remote—
    When, startled by strange tidings, she in haste
    Burst wide the mighty banquet-hall where feast
A thousand lords about the King, all wrought
To maddening din—till, lo ! what trembling smote
    The sacred vessels, fetched by fell behest,
    And lift to impious lips 'mid scornful jest,
Whilst on the wall Heaven's mystic fingers wrote ?
    From guest to guest spread horror ! Pale he sat
The glittering despot, fixed in ghostly stare,
    Reckless of pride, or shame, or royal state,
A prisoner at his own dread judgment bar—
'Though none could read the writing, he read there
    Himself—God's vessel—darkly desecrate !

BETHESDA.

Thirty-and-eight years !   Yet still by the spring
  Of healing waters, helpless and forlorn,
He watched full oft the angel's flashing wing
  Charged with Heaven's dewy splendours past him
     borne,
While startled depths once more shot eddying
  (Only to wake again fair hope forsworn !)
That widening web of waters' glittering ring,
  Sealing once more life's doom wrecked soon as
     born.
But patient disappointment yet shall win,
  Hope's pitiful despair a God shall woo—
Wilt be made whole ?   And Love straight put him in
  That fountain veiled in Calvary's dark death-dew !
Faith's long blind gaze at last rent Heaven rewards,—
Such triumphs still the Book of Life records.

THE MAN OF SORROWS.

Did the great Master weep? We know He wept,
  Yea, wept aloud o'er lost Jerusalem,
That wrapt in purple pride of evening slept
    Unconscious of Rome's ploughshare through her
      dream.
    Again at Bethany, what power could stem
Love's sinless soul-drops from His eyes that leapt?
    And did not His whole body weep, I deem—
Weep blood—whilst horror through the olives crept !

But did the Man of Sorrows never smile?
    Ask yon torn cliff by fiery anguish riven,
    Sparkling with glittering storm-drops off it driven,
If childhood's innocence did ne'er beguile
From those worn lips—that first spelt out " Forgiven"
To desperate souls—new wonder-light from Heaven !

MARY AT THE SEPULCHRE.

Night's orphaned heavens slow faded sphere on
    sphere,
  The dews of natural sleep lay on the ground
  As healing earth's dark supernatural wound,
Faint dawn now kept new sabbath without fear.
'Mid yon hushed garden's perfumed precincts, where
  The sleeping boughs spring-music hold fast bound,
  What twilight form in haste peers round and round,
Searching death's rifled, stingless sepulchre ?
  'Tis Mary weeping o'er the empty tomb,
Weeping for her lost Lord so late laid dead ;
  Tear-blind, though dazzling angels fill His room—
He speaks !—'twas as the sun's majestic head,
  That soared in pomp and splendour o'er night
    gloom,
Stooped from high heaven to dry one dew-drenched
    weed !

ST. JOHN IN PATMOS.

And art Thou He, my Lord, my very Lord,
  Who drew me out of darkness into light,
  And loved me to Himself with infinite
And sweet entanglement of look and word,
Waking lost nature like some magic chord?
  Lo, now Thou stand'st all soul! unearthly bright!
  Such holiness is death to mortal sight,
Such Deity too high to be adored!
  Art Thou indeed the Christ, the Christ who died!-
On whose dear breast I leaned that night of shame,
  When He outside the fold, alone outside,
Met the destroying angel—stricken Lamb!—
  And dark Gethsemane left glorified,
And Calvary's lintel blood-writ with His Name?

ASCENSION MORNING.

WHO recognised the Christ that wondrous morn
   Love's sad feet last trod lost Jerusalem ?
   Did Pilate start ?—'twas he I did condemn,
Pathetic Prince to no earth-purple born !
Or she, dream-haunted, who 'mid Hebrew scorn
   Dashed in with piteous warnings learnt in dream ?
   Barabbas ? snatched from felon's rude cross-beam
By Innocence in diadem of thorn !
   Wake, guilty Salem, wake !   Love lingers yet—
Soon, soon Gethsemane brings back to view,
   In spite of day, white moonlight, bloody sweat !
When lo ! Ascension's sunny stair bursts through,
   And heavenward urged by beckoning Olivet,
Christ waves green Bethany a last adieu !

THE CROSS, THE TREE OF LIFE.

O wondrous Tree, that blossomed 'mid eclipse,
   Whose sanguine clusters ripened in no sun
   But infinite dark, ere glory scarce begun
To kiss sin's mountain-tops with faint gold lips !
Lo ! now the fearless Dove's white pinion slips
   Through those forsaken arms that victory won,
   Transplanted by omnipotence—'Tis done !—
'Mid central blaze of Heaven's Apocalypse.
   Though rude earth's trellis, yet the immortal Vine
Her bursting buds stretched darkling down Time's
      slope,
   To catch last rays of Mercy's sun's decline
And treasure them for all the seed of hope ;
   Till purple clusters, brimmed with Heaven's glad
      wine,
Shame Eshcol's vale, and with lost Eden cope !

"I AM WITH YOU ALWAY."

Thou great "I am" still with me! O what strength,
What fellowship in that o'ershadowing fame!
Angels that wait on Thee will ask my name,
And wonder Thou dost commune at such length
With creature so unworthy! Tell them, Lord,
I was a poor dependent once of Thine,
With name so tarnished that Thou saidst, Take
Mine,
And bid'st me to Thy house and heart and board!
"I am" of all the ages!—Thou'rt the same
That walked with prophet and with patriarch
In the world's twilight, while it yet was dark,—
Creation's dawn fresh echoing back, "I am"!
Twilight and dark still linger here—O call,
Call home my proud will, life's last prodigal!

THE ARK.

As when of old the man whose name was Rest,
  Searching the watery waste from sky to sky,
  The Ark's sole window oped, and noiselessly
Fair fluttering forth upon her solemn quest,
The dove slid fondly from the Patriarch's breast —
    So, ere dread Calvary's death-floods scarce were
        dry,
    Heaven's window oped, and, fire-crowned from on
        high,
The Spirit Dove descends to be man's guest.
And so again at death, the ark once more—
    Life's fragile ark that's breasted many a wave,
Though pirate storm on storm besieged the door
    In vain waylaying Heaven's fair inmate brave—
    Her lattice yields,—and swift, dew-glistering, grave
The white-winged spirit seeks Love's sunlit shore !

THE GOSPEL DRAW-NET.

There is a Kingdom with God's favour fair,
  Luring lost souls to its sublime embrace,
Which the Great Master doth Himself compare
  To some vast draw-net, that, cast forth o'er space
Of Time's night-wandering waters, with slow care
  Garners rich quarry from the watery chase,
Surprising it unhurt and unaware
  In Love's delicious toils of deathless grace.
Ye meshes of strong mercy, knotted close
  With knots of justice, first 'mid startled shoals
Deep sunk 'neath Calvary's death-weights, whence up-
      rose,
  Buoyant, brave life-floats that outride Time's
      goals —
  Sift, sift wild waters for their wealth of souls,
While angels land them where no tempest blows !

CROSS-BEARING.

Some meek souls wear Christ's yoke serenely well,
    And bear triumphantly the load of life,
    Lie still beneath the Husbandman's keen knife,
And find in weights wings scarce invisible.
And some heroic souls life's wounds impel—
    Press awful on, 'mid pauses in the strife,
    And wed the cross as others woo a wife,
And win fresh glory where so late they fell.
Speak, ye that Freedom's heights sublimely know,
    And tread with brave feet all life's chequered
        land,
He who o'er dark Gethsemane could sing,
First bowed His will like some majestic bow,
    And placed it strung within His Father's hand,
Thence all the purposes of Heaven took wing !

SELF-FORGETFULNESS.

High saints of God, there's yet a higher height,
   Where God's great Son reveals Himself unveiled
   To yearning souls in innocency mailed,
Like pale night-dews surprised by morning light !
'Tis not attained by victor faith, in spite
   Of summits inaccessible fresh scaled,
   Nor burning zeal though dauntless, hell-assailed—
Fair self-oblivion is that region bright !
Ye bowed saints, long by fearfulness bereaved
   Of your own saintship, trembling to offend,
Still testing faith lest Self should be deceived,
   Staining Truth's mirror over which ye bend
With the hot breath of penitence, yet grieved
   For cold grief—Ah ! 'tis sun-kissed dews ascend !

LIFE'S DAY.

FIRST beauty stole from out the wings of night,
   And flung a luminous joy o'er all the land,
   Blessing and praise then linking hand in hand,
Earth, sea, and sky together worshipped light.
God of the light, to Thee I lift mine eyes,
   To Thee in gratitude I bend my knees,
   Thy folded wings brought down star-mysteries,
But the unfolding lifts me to the skies !
O mystery of earth, dim isle sea-lost !
   O wondrous being lived in Time's full gale !
O age on age fresh darkening death's salt strand !
Life is but one long journey to the coast,
   Death is the pier from which our life sets sail,
And as we lade our vessels so we land !

SPIRIT FULNESS.

As up yon mountain-side, past field on field
   Ascending, wall-enclosed, flocks onward press
   Towards open fells, which, stretching limitless,
Free to the mountain summit pasture yield—
So strong pure souls shall find, once Spirit-filled,
   Wide open heavenward boundless promises !—
   Expanding evermore past storm and stress
Towards freedom's heights, where faith's rock-eagles
      build.

Wide open heavenward lie all Truth's fair lands—
   And though our poor words measure and confine
   Whilst they convey the grape-blood of the Vine,
God's words have hid wings faith's warm touch ex-
      pands.
Our empty souls when filled like vessels sink
Of their own fulness in the flood they drink.

FOUR TYPICAL WRESTLERS IN HOLY WRIT

FOUR TYPICAL WRESTLERS IN HOLY WRIT

JACOB AT PENIEL.

" Hushed are my people now ; the tents' low peaks,
Gathered in groups within the dewy hollow,
Stand thick with moonlight.   Rest thee, Innocence !
No sound now breaks the stillness that extends
From my lone feet up through the infinite heavens,
Through night's interminable waste of stars
That round heaven's gate seem folded like a flock—
God's flock of worlds now folded for the night—
Up to the silent Throne !   Yea, all is hushed
Save my tumultuous heart that toils and rests not,
Tilling the unprofitable soil of hope,
Like murmuring Jabbok chafing at my feet.
How the tense stillness presses on my spirit,
And with intolerable pause the populous heavens
Seem hushed through their illimitable ranks,
Like hosts before the battle.   O for one
To rend their stately ranks, and stir the stillness
With the unutterable voice of God

Commanding in the midst !   O worlds, ye know not
What makes me dark 'mid your far leagues of light
Quivering along your pulses.   The stern shadow
Of my avenging brother haunts my life,—
My brother, whom I injured guilefully,
Filching a father's blessing from his brow,
And binding it untruthfully to mine,
In youth's mad eagerness to disappoint
The obscure destiny of later birth.
Mad stealth ! where is my father's blessing now ?
I stole a curse, and lo ! it clings to me ;
It clasps my clammy temples, chills my blood
With fear's unnatural frost I never knew.
My blessing was a curse in such disguise
As I disguised myself to overreach
My blind old father, not so blind as I.
And evermore I suck the bitterness
Of those unholy gains,—that luscious lie ;
And evermore the long unburied years
Rise up against me, hedge in all my ways,
And crush me with their frowning, till I lie
Engulfed in my own greatness cunningly !
How the lie shook me, when those feeble fingers
Wandered about me doubtfully and solemn,
When those worn hands, with hesitating warmth,

Like the spent rays of winter's feeble sunset,
Gathered at last to rest upon my brow,
Betrayed into a blessing undeserved,—
Yet from that day to this still unrelinquished,
Perchance to be a blessing when I die.
How oft in dreams I feel that wasted touch,
Heavy with prophecy, and fraught with power,
Far reaching down my life !   The tremulous shadows
Of those blind fingers still play o'er my brow
Blindly,—still shadow my too chequered life.
My hard-won flocks and herds, I hear them still
Journeying to meet him, to appease his face—
My brother Esau—Esau, the great prince,
Who comes against me with four hundred men,
Are those his armèd hoofs I catch from far ?"

Then, like one slain outright with sudden terror,
The patriarch fell full length upon his face
Prone in the dust, and as he lay and panted,
All the hushed earth lay listening round his spirit,
And heaven, to shut him in with sympathy,
O'ershadowed him with cloud ; and in the storm
Of strong remorse, his life quick came and went
In fitful struggle, as when one in haste
Bears against fitful night a kindling torch :

So sharp the gusts of memory smote upon him,
And, burying him in ruins of himself,
So beat upon him that he could not rise,
Till far beyond the horizon of his past,
Clouded with falsehood, the great world's horizon
Encompassed him in its tremendous grasp;
And beyond this again a ring of light
Compassed the world, and a low voice from Eden
Sounded quite near him : " It shall bruise thy head
Thou serpent tempter, with thy false, false tongue."
And suddenly the woman's holy seed
Stood imaged in his soul,—another Adam,
Tempted but not seduced, the perfect Man
Bruised in His flesh, but whose unbroken life
Of perfect holiness, should yet absorb
Into Himself sin and its sting for ever.

" What if of me," he cried unto himself,—
" What if of me be born the woman's Seed,
To bury all my falsehood in His truth,
And live for all men truth before high God !
For so at Luz God spoke to me at midnight,
On such a night as this (it thrills me now—
Twenty long years are fled, but still it fades not !),
When first self-outlawed, stretched on rocky waste,

The heavens stooped o'er me, and huge stars like
    souls
Leaned out of heaven, full orbed ; and suddenly
A swift bright ladder, like a royal ray
Shot from the inner throne, stood at my feet,
Trembling with light ; and on it messengers,
O'er it a voice, for down the love-thronged stair
God's near voice spake : ' In thee and in thy seed
Shall all the families of earth be blessed.'
I could not be deceived ; much less could God
Deceive an outcast in his bitterest hour.
That voice I've heard in secret through long years,
'Twas like a hidden fire for faith to run to,
God-lit, 'mid frosts of night and worse of friends :
That voice, I say, I've heard throughout long years,
Still follow it in vain.   I hear it now,
That self-same voice : ' In thee and in thy seed
Shall all the families of earth be blessed.'
Impossible ! and I go still unblessed,
Or rather clogged with blessing as I go,—
Blessed with a curse !   If ever I meet God
As then at Luz (well might I call it Bethel,
For God kept open house for me that night,
Far on the homeless plain !) at once I'll tell Him,
In spite of blessing I am still unblessed.

I'll ask Him then and there, with His own hands,
If what He said be true, Himself to bless me ;
I'll never let Him go until He does it.
I am resolved I will at last break open
This mystic blessing, even if I die.
I've borne this blessed burden long enough,
I cannot bear it more.   Could I but see Him
Once, once again ; but must I needs despair,
Since those fair angels met me this same morn
At Mahanaim, God's great unseen host,
Marching to Heaven's low music through the wild,
To camp about His children !   Not by chance—
It could not be—God's escort met me first,
Ere I got news of Esau's armèd band
Travelling to crush me,—where God's angels come,
He's sure to follow !   God, long injured, now
Melts me with mercy ; the great God forgives !
Yea, the great God forgives, forgives, forgives
The meanest, vilest, worst !   This is the word
Twenty slow years have barely now spelt out
Before my wondering eyes,—free, free forgiveness
To faithless ones, heart-smitten, who still dare
Mercy's lone depths to sound ; nor shrink again
Life's folds, where long dead sins secrete themselves
Corrupting, to expose to Love's pure gaze,

Whate'er it cost.   O God, Thou saidst that night,
While all my sin fresh stared me in the face,
Words ringing in my conscience all life since,
' I'll surely do thee good ;' then do it, Lord,
Now, for Thou know'st I need it !   I believe,
Yea, love Thee in this dark, if Thou wilt have it,
Vile as I am.   Show me the Blessed Seed :
O for a voice, a word, a look, a light !"—

While thus his mind felt darkly down the future,
Craving the dawn of that long-promised day
Of man's deliverance, he unconsciously
Half-raised himself, and, propped upon his knees,
Fell in upon himself, and cried to Heaven
For pardon to obliterate his sin—
False sin, till, lifted by his agony,
And the intenser tempest raging in him,
He struggled to his feet, and with high arms
Cast forth upon the solitary air,
Far straining upward toward the infinite
He groped for God, if haply he might find Him,
And lean his burdened spirit right upon Him,
And wrest an instant blessing ; so he groped,
Grappling the solitude, and lo ! 'twas God.
For, unperceived, the God-man stood beside him,

And, answering palpably his importunate arms,
He grasped him in return, and, grappling with him,
Long locked lost Jacob in His living arms.

For so God waits in solitary places
And wastes of life, in terror's haunted plains—
Prayer's thronging hush, and in each narrow pass
And dark retirement of soul-chastisement—
Lurks in the dusk to waylay desperate souls
Craving to meet Him, murmuring to come near Him
Who yet perchance most irresistibly
Stumble against Him in the dark of sin ;
Albeit for this they go halt all their days,
Yet they've got at Him, wrung His secret from Him,
And wear it in their bosom till they die.

Thus by omnipotence surprised, embraced,
Jacob long wrestled, nor did all the weight
Of God Himself yet break the bruisèd reed,
So tender is His multitudinous strength ;
But as some father tempting his least child
To conquer him with weakness, craving love,
Puts back the first wild impotence of strength,
Then strongly yields to his redoubled effort,—
So he, the o'ershadowing Angel closing round him,

Found the lone dark alive, and wrestled with it.
Mysterious strife ! the dumb intensity
Awed the hushed night ; God seemed now to rehearse
His own Gethsemane ; the dark hours fled
To bring the dawn ; when suddenly a cry,
More strangely human than earth ever heard,
Out of the struggling darkness, " Let me go."

Let me go !—'twas thus the heavenly Wrestler,
Petitioning against His creature's power
Put forth upon Him irresistibly,
Sued for release.   O prayer, what bonds are these !
Can these thy shameless arms cast round thy Lord
Arrest His goings, fetter His great freedom,
Enclose His boundless pity with thy wants,
And care's entangling network ?   Bind Him then,—
Bind Him to thee with subtle influences
Sweeter than Pleiades, with surer coils
Than e'er hell's serpent wove ! O prayer, enthrall
      Him,
Till God becomes thy suppliant : " Let me go,
For the day breaketh."—Nay, not so, my Lord !
For this same cause, till day break on my soul,
I will not let Thee go except Thou bless me ;
And blessing, Thou wilt never let me go.

God's prayer unanswered ?   Lord, Thy suit denied !
Thou whose all-sovereign voice uprose to heaven,
"Father, I will !"   And shall a halt child cry
Out of His guilty darkness, " I will not !
Let the day break,—my heart's already broken ;
Self I abandon, but Thee never, Lord !"
And Thou didst own him, yea, encourage him
With instant honour,—him whom Thou hadst smitten,
Dislodging in a moment his bold strength
Proudly rebellious, till Thy vanquished one,
Falling right on Thee with his sin's full weight,
Clinging about Thy greatness, like crushed flowers
That spend themselves upon the foot that crushed
     them,
Cleaving in perfume,—stricken he prevails !
Foreshadowing darkly, though in sin's disguise,—
Foreshadowing, O earth, thy stainless Flower
Down-trodden on the cross, yet filling heaven
With piercèd Love's new odours !   And for us
Now, and for all, through centuries of night,
Stands forth alive Heaven's mystic parable,—
The human and divine commingling,—life
Evolving out of death,—a human Hand
Bearing aloft through sin's dark night of waves,
Undimmed, God's blessing to crown lost ones' brows !

That cry thrilled wondering Jacob : " Let me go,
For the day breaketh : therefore let me go."
" Nay, nay, my Lord ; why tarry not till dawn?
Why shun the light ?   One thing that cry hath taught
    me,—
Thou great Unseen ! though my antagonist,
Thou canst not leave me till I give thee leave.
I will constrain Thee : wherefore shall rude day
Break off my soul's espousals at their height ?
Love is imperious—Tarry, or else here
Pledge me Thy name for ever."
                        But to these,
His spirit's inner strivings, none replied,
Save, " Wherefore is it thou dost ask My name ?"
Yet afterward he knew as though God spake.—
In the free life of faith, sight seeth not ;
Faith steps upon the word,—her only " seen ";
Faith wings invisible air, and though 'tis night,
Faith's starry eyes grow larger in the dark,
And with unnatural splendour pierce the gloom.
Unheard at midnight, Faith embarks her all
Upon some ancient promise of the Word,
Blind sense discarding.   After bootless toil,
Hers the fair morning-shore, where none durst ask,
Who art thou ?—miracles so take the breath.

Faith unsupported walks the dark, nor craves
Like questioning Jacob doubting his own touch,
What is thy name? who art thou? knowing well,
Even in the darkness, Love's familiar voice,—
The voice of my Beloved!   Love's quick ears
Chide tedious sight.   Behold, behold, He cometh!
Mountains can't hide Him.   Thou hast heard, hast
    felt,
Handling with mortal hands the unseen God,—
" Blessed are they that see not, yet believe !"—
And there He blessed him.   The same hand that
    smote,
Now blessed ; for all who touch the lowest hem,
Find in the dust access to Deity.

    Thus at life's turning-point, when now at length
His dark days wheeled into the sudden light,
As kings who knight upon the battle-field
The boldest in the onset, so the Lord
New-named His victor, now no longer Jacob,
Clandestinely usurping life's prime boon,
But Israel now,—most honourable prince,
For ever vested with invisible powers,—
Powers of the world to come !   For lo ! henceforth
To beg is kingly, yea, upon thy knees
To wield the sceptre of a want, a cry,

Is sovereignty high God cannot resist,
But hearkens to obey.   Thus crowned He him
First of the royal line of mightiest kings,
Prince of the sons of prayer by right divine.
Let Edom boast proud Esau's sons her dukes
Israel, thou mighty wrestler, prince with God
And fellow-men, thou hast indeed prevailed.
For lo ! God bows Himself from heaven's great
　　height
Submissive to thy grasp,—yea, sues from thee,
As from a sovereign, terms of His surrender ;
And now behold thy brother, whom thou fearedst
Through the long years, whose face thou dream'dst on
　　flame,
Travelling against thee with an armèd host,
To slay thee and thy treachery together,—
Behold thy brother Esau, clad in kindness,
Bright with the morning, runneth forth to greet thee,
Falls on thy neck with kisses and hot tears,
(Smit by one sun, stern hearts soon flow together),
Folding thee in a brother's free forgiveness !—
O prince with God and men, thou hast prevailed !
Scarce had He blessed him there unspeakably,
When sudden daybreak, leaping on the plain,
Broke o'er him dazzling ; but lo ! He was gone,—

He who with him had travailed wondrously
Through the long night to that fair edge of dawn,
Leaving him flushed with sunrise and new spoils !

But lo ! the gold of dawn had lost its colour :
Henceforth to him the night outshone the day.
And evermore his soul sought sorrowing,
Night after night, throughout whole years of nights,
Another night like that which shamed the dawn,
And left a faded lustre over all.
And oft, lone spirit, out upon the plain
He knelt and watched, what time, earth held in still
  ness,
Evening's long splendours smote the lonely hills :—
Or Day ebbed fire, and draining dark the world,
Bared the great bed of heaven to its far deeps,
And shuddering shoals of unextinguished stars
Fresh bathed in brightness ; treasures unreleased
Till night's return ; immeasurable shores,
New shining evermore, yet undiscovered
Till God puts out the candle of the world !
And still he lingered, and yet ever vain
His utmost searchings, for still night was night,
Darker for disappointment and day-dreams.
Fair earth's familiar haunts, and heaven's lit plains,

Once near, seemed lone as ocean solitudes
And the long travelling tremor of far seas.
Thus worn with hollow hunger of desire,
Oft communed he with Death inquiringly--—
O Death, thou night of nights, last brightest hope,
Break, break this lock of life, and let me to Him,
As night unlocks the secrets of the skies !
O Death, what worlds lie hid within thy shadow !
Like miser night, thou hoardest in thy bosom
What dar'st not count till darkness shuts thee in !
And oft he dashed the sunrise from his eyes,
As something that obscured his hungering gaze,
So hungered he for visions of the night ;
And more than visions, revelations near
Of unseen fellowship,—that strange sweet strength
Put forth against him suddenly and long,
Encompassing his weakness ; the live pressure
Of infinite Love Himself, God's shining secret
Revealed, yet unrevealed, once and no more.

Soul hunger eats God's image into life,
Soul hunger is the noblest death to die.

'Tis life to see God face to face in Christ,
Therefore the patriarch called it Peniel.

Not to see God, yet follow Him, is Faith,
Therefore the Lord came not to him again.
Not to see God, yet, if He smite, to cling,
Is Faith's fair flower that still lights many a waste ;
God consecrates it still with His new name.
Not to see God, although we have lived with Him,
And yet to worship Him whom we have lost,
This is Faith's vintage, and yields royal wine !
' It is expedient that I go away,'
Christ said, and soaring opened wide Heaven's gate,
For by the ladder of the wounded Christ
Faith climbs unhurt the heights of Deity.

———

THE SYROPHENICIAN MOTHER.

IT is my Mother's story, let me tell
It over now she's gone ; each syllable
Seems burnt upon my brain—her very tone :—
It is my Mother's story—and my own !

Meanwhile within this woodland wilderness,
Where Spring, soft crowding, heals each rent recess

'Mid rippling roof, and breezy labyrinth
Of lighted leaves, rest on this fall'n oak plinth
Stretched 'mid a sapphire sea of hyacinth,
That, crowned with floating sapphire mist, low broods
Like heaven's blue stillness carpeting the woods.
Lo, winter's past indeed, the rains are gone,
And, buried deep, the turtle's happy moan
And mellow murmur comes on breezes blown,
All earth tells out her teeming parable—
And Mother's story to His praise I'll tell !

" Born in the dark of heathendom, alone,
A mother, yet no mother, from my own—
My only ' own,' my child, (as if all hell
Lay gulfed betwixt us) Satan's demon spell
Had banished me, though close beside her, far,—
Far from my life's lone treasure, my sole star
That shone within my widowed home, and lit
My night with hope—till now I sit and sit,
The silence more intense because she moves
And lives and clings,—and yet lives not nor loves.
O God, Great Spirit, whom I dare not see,
Yet dare to challenge in the dark, I flee
Out of my awful stillness into Thine
Unknown more awful stillness, to break mine !

As when a pain I could no longer bear
I've stilled with deeper pain without a tear,
So from despair's long dark against Thy dark
More terrible, I'll strike as 'twere a spark
Of deeper darkness, and lie down and die,
And spend my whole life's breath in one last cry.

*   *   *   *   *

A Prophet who can walk the sea, and raise
The very dead !—I'll die but I will gaze
Upon that wondrous face that talks with God,
And though 'twere twice as far, my precious load
I'll carry in Faith's arms—Love has strong arms,
But Faith has stronger !—past all doubt's alarms,
And lay her down, although invisible
To others' gaze, where His pure eyes shall dwell
In their full summer on my child's pale wreck,
Till life's full tide, obeying His high beck,
Shall lift her back to life, and her wild eyes
Shall rest in mine with new-born love's surprise !
I'll have but once to lay my secret bare,
At once I know He'll answer my despair ;
I know He'll walk my sorrow's sea, and brave
Depths worse than death to break her living grave
And her poor mother, thus when she has won
Her trampled blossom back, fair in the sun

Expanding her live petals in my sight,
Leaning each languid leaf against the light,
Will plant it in His bosom with one cry—
'Tis my sole flower, it burst beneath Thy sky,
Wear it, Great Lord, henceforth ! content I die."

Here for a moment Mother used to pause,
Not to draw breath—no, that was not the cause ;
Her absent look invariably confessed
Some broken vow crept back into her breast ;
A sudden stillness stood within her eye,
As if some door of gladness she'd passed by
And never could find more, howe'er she strove—
The joy of giving to the one we love.
For haunting still to waylay and annoy,
Here Memory met her, and would taunts employ,
Still cradling in bright arms hope's withered joy.
But she vain sobbing, " Christ, come back again,
That faithless vow consumes my soul with pain,
All, all is Thine henceforth !"—resumed her strain.

" Tear-worn and travel-worn, I came at length,
Pressed   through   the   crowd   with   all   my   failing
        strength,
Lifted my voice on high with wailings wild—
' Have mercy on me, Lord ! my only child

Is tortured with a devil'—but none stirred,
He looked, indeed, but answered not a word.
Listening all over to catch the first sound,
I dug my desperate knees into the ground ;
Silence so insupportable, intense,
Bereft my being of all other sense —
As when, storm-hung, low darkening thunder-lands,
Hushed in   sublime   suspense,   stretch   thirsting
      hands—
Earth,   Hell,   both   leagued   against   me !   but   now
      worse,
Worse than hell's ghastly guest, or Canaan's curse,
My one faint hope, one window toward the sky,
That gleamed athwart my night of destiny,
Like some high midnight lattice glimmering pale,
Burnished with fitful moonlight's mystic mail,—
This now was blinded with the beating rain
Of my own tears, and shrouded every pane !
The Man of Mercy I thought Heaven had sent
To seek lost souls, but seals my banishment
With cruel silence?   God hates, it is clear,—
Hates   me, —yes, me.   Hush,   goading   heart—for
      bear ;
Perchance He heard not,—then in stronger tone
I wept my sorrow louder—He moved on—

I followed, all my being in a flame
Of mad intensity, beyond all shame
Of heartless men who spurned me pleading thus,
' Send her away, she crieth after us.'
These His disciples, too ! who must have known
A woman's anguish, thus shut out alone
As I was ; but (God pardon my complaint)
This broke at last His silence—' I'm not sent
But to lost sheep of chosen Israel.'
What could He mean ? That first word tolled the knell
Of all my hopes.   My heart, till now all fire,
Turned white with ashes of burnt-out desire.
What could a poor dark heathen woman know
Of God's mysterious sovereignty ?   Although
I did know this, if God be sovereign good,
The darkest soul might on His light intrude
And yet be guiltless, if he seek the light
To strip sin bare, not make it falsely bright.
What could I do ?   A thought flashed through my
    brain :
He's sent, He says, to seek lost sheep—that's plain—
I'm a lost sheep, maybe I'll yet prevail,
Lost sheep—most true, but not of Israel !
That moment I remembered oft I'd heard,
How Israel first by prayer o'ercame his Lord—

Then without look or murmur, sound or sigh,
One sudden bound—and at His feet I lie,
A second Israel ! ' Help, Lord,' all I said—
And pillowing on those dusty feet my head,
I worshipped as I wept, yea, wept and worshippèd

" Of course I knew I was no Israel,
He was a mighty prince, I knew full well ;
He knelt upon God's promise, but I found
Each step I trespassed on forbidden ground ;
He to o'ercome his brother dared the deed,
Satan himself my foe—far direr need ;
Nature's blind instinct upward my wild plea,
A mother's love my sole divinity !
Then from Heaven's height to me, prone at
      feet,
At last this word descended—' 'Tis not meet
To take the children's bread and cast to dogs.'
' Yes, Lord,' I gasped, and lo ! as when white fogs
Lift from rain-sodden lands to greet the sun—
Hope ghostly rose ! and I, who lay undone,
Felt I had conquered by divine despair
Christ's utmost silence : for to me down there,
To me, not His disciples now, He spoke,
To me myself, and thus deliverance broke—

' Yes, Lord, and yet wouldst Thou refuse a crumb
The children may let fall to a poor dumb
Expectant dog, soul-hunger forced to come !'
No place too low for me to occupy,
'Twas this I meant : Lord, low in dust I lie—
And yet I meant, too, there's no place too low
For Mercy to stoop down to, Lord, I know.
But as I spake amazement bowed my mind,
How thus I dared to challenge Him in kind ;
For something in His bearing greatly awed
And overcame me, as if I saw God !
Yet He was plain as any desert flower
None heeds, till suddenly at sunset hour
It starts, transfigured, at your feet !—I turned,
And thought His face like some far seraph's burned !

" But that mysterious word, ' the children's bread,'
Filled me with wonder, darkening all He said ;
And yet I felt hope slept within that gloom,
As soft-gloomed April, brooding, lifts the bloom
It seemed to crush, and liberates perfume.
' The children's bread '—what could He mean ?   I'c
  come
To fetch Him to drive Satan from my home.
How can I give thee children's bread ? He cries,—

O God ! how dark are all Heaven's mysteries !
Must not, then, 'children's bread' be some strange
    charm
To drive out Satan—heal his deadly harm ?
And every household child, by right divine,
Has children's bread ! Would God that right were mine !
How Christ must long that every child would eat
The children's bread, nor suffer more defeat !
Something of this fled whirling through my mind—
Some bright, unworded, wonder undefined,
Whose sudden flash and flicker left me blind !
No place too low for me to occupy,
Was all I seemed to see :—Lord ! low I lie,
And yet I felt there is no place too low
For Mercy to stoop down to—this I know.
Prostrate I lay and listened on the ground,—
Dust is the best conductor of far sound,
As every shepherd knows who bows his ear,
Lower and lower, the lost bleat to hear.
'Twas but a moment, but it seemed long hours,
So fast the soul lives,—when, past mortal powers,
At once all Heaven brake over me, and I,
Taught by some sudden instinct from the sky,
Knew I had conquered Christ's severity.
And such a rush of revelation came,

I lost myself, and saw but His great name.
'Lost sheep' no more, how could I be so bold?
I, a lost sheep, who never knew a fold,
Nor shepherd e'er knew me—truth, Lord, indeed,
A heathen dog! this, this my righteous meed.
On her poor mother's head lie all the blame,
Mine was the guilt that brought on her the
  shame.
Breathless I lay "—(here Mother's starting eyes
Betrayed some bursting dawn of wild surprise
We saw not!)—" when, Great God, oh, strangely
  sweet,
Sounds like the voice of hidden waters greet
And quench my ears' long thirst—submerged all
  guilt—
'O woman, great thy faith, even as thou wilt
Now be it unto thee!' And from that hour
My daughter was made whole by instant power.

"How I got home I know not, this I know—
'Twas life to linger, but 'twas life to go!
And how I found her laid upon the bed
Stunned with strange joy, till, starting at my tread,
She bounded forth, and met me at the door,
With resurrection dews all sparkling o'er—

Like morn's first sunlit branch escaped the night,
That breathless drinks bright draughts of quivering
       light—
All dew and lustre, bloom and blossom now,
Wings in her feet, and sunrise on her brow,
And sweeter far to me than all beside—
Her free voice thrilled the heavens that eventide !

" So while the sunset died along the hills,
And twilight earth lay listening to her rills,
I, step by step, told o'er my wondrous way—
Prayer's long ascent from darkness into day,
And as I ceased she faltered : ' Mother, pray.' "

Was ever any mother blessed like mine ?
She craved a crumb, He brought forth Heaven's best
       wine :—
She like a dog lay down to kiss His feet,
He grandly stooped and crowned her in the street :—
Her hunger broke into God's stores of grace,
He fed upon the famine of her face,
And flinging open wide Heaven's granary-door,
" Even as thou wilt," He said,—what more, what
       more ?
And ever after as the years rolled on,

If e'er distress had saddened mother's tone,
I called to mind this wondrous word of His—
"O woman, great thy faith !" and how with this—
God's silence, sovereignty, severity,
(Of Heaven's dread body-guard the ghostliest three !)
With prayer's one single weapon she o'ercame,
And won herself and me a deathless name.
Then, creeping to her side, I kissed her cheek,
And said to her, although I could not speak,—
" He's the same mighty Saviour still to-day,
And Prayer is mighty still! O mother, pray !"

GETHSEMANE.

I.

WHAT supernatural stillness awes to-night
  The antient Garden of the Olive-press ?
White light like moral moonlight fiercely bright
  Searches with holiness each dim recess.
But list, 'mid echoes of the Paschal hymn
  Whose rugged Hebrew chant falls plaintive here,
What voice serene as 'mid the Seraphim—
  " Bind, bind the sacrifice with cords "—rings clear ?

But now, ah! see beneath yon shadowing boughs,
   Hushed as if listening for lost steps in Heaven,
What prostrate bleeding Form with desperate vows
   Pleads as against some dreaded cup now given
Mid awful dialogue where none replies—
Till lo, through hell's gloom Love's swift Angel flies!

II.

Awful impossibility of Love!
   And was there no response to that dread cry,
   "If it be possible"? that rent the sky—
None—from the boundless Father-Heart above?
No voice of Thine, Thou bright baptismal Dove,
   Who seal'dst that brow with solemn augury,
   None for that same grand Soul now doomed to die,
Rent by two worlds that in His bosom strove?
Impossible! 'Twas echoed from the Throne,
   Mid awful hush of angels' quivering strings :—
Impossible! All Hades gave a groan,
   And shuddering shades shook ghost-light from their
      wings.
Impossible! justice and guilt make moan,
   Impossible! the dying saint low sings.

ST. PAUL'S THORN IN THE FLESH.

'Αρκει σοι ἡ χαρις μου : "My grace is sufficient for thee
2 COR. xii. 9.

A VOICE, a vision through the haze
   Of Time's long vista greets me now,
Saints down the ages turn and gaze—
   'Tis 'Αρχει σοι ἡ χαρις μου.

With thorn-pierced flesh and trembling knees,
   Mighty Apostle—is it thou
Whose faint brow craves no mortal breeze?
   List ! 'Αρχει σοι ἡ χαρις μου.

But look again—O prayer-rent sky !
   O deathless breeze ! O lighted brow !
Now welcome Pain's dark mystery !
   Since 'Αρχει σοι ἡ χαρις μου.

Thrice wrestling with the self-same plea,
   Thrice did the mighty suppliant bow ;
Saints still have their Gethsemane—
   Still 'Αρχει σοι ἡ χαρις μου.

Ye struggling souls that cannot rise,
   Encumbered with blind Whence and How,
Here's a new promise from the skies—
   God's 'Αρχει σοι ἡ χαρις μου.

Heaven's bright new promise, flashing far,
   Hangs beckoning on Truth's lowest bough !
Thorns henceforth have their own bright star,
   'Tis 'Αρχει σοι ἡ χαρις μου.

That single thorn, dropt from the Crown
   Of thorns that wreathed the Master's brow,
Still triumph to torn saints brings down—
   Still 'Αρχει σοι ἡ χαρις μου.

Five victor-wounds the Christ still bears,
   Five porches for sick souls, I trow,
Whose thorns for palms He grandly wears,
   While 'Αρχει σοι ἡ χαρις μου.

Here gloriously to faith are met
  Man's boundless need, God's boundless Now,
Each to each other tuned and set
  In Ἀρκεῖ σοι ἡ χάρις μου.

Wants are but empty vessels, Lord,
  For Thee to fill—Faith asks not how,
But fearless waits Thy sovereign Word,
  Heaven's Ἀρκει σοι ἡ χάρις μου.

As seabirds haunt on snowy wings
  The fretted cliff's dark riven brow,
Grace builds in Nature's wants and sings
  Her Ἀρκει σοι ἡ χάρις μου.

Ah, white-winged Grace that wandering came
  O'er Time's wild sea—Thou, only Thou
Couldst Sin's dark clefts of sorrow claim
  With Ἀρκει σοι ἡ χάρις μου.

All-conquering Grace, thee, thee I own,
  Enough for all, enough for now,
Weakness thy workshop, thorns thy throne,
  For Ἀρκει σοι ἡ χάρις μου.

O haunting voice of Christ my Lord !
   Through foes and fears and faithless vow
I'll hew my way with this one sword—
   Truth's Ἀρχει σοι ἡ χαρις μου.

O haunting Voice for ever near,
   Ring out 'mid din of sword and plough,
Through Faith's keen frosty air ring clear
   Love's Ἀρχει σοι ἡ χαρις μου !

SONNETS AND OTHER PIECES

IN MEMORIAM.

EPITAPHS.

Each man writes his own epitaph each day,
This the unconscious business of our lives—
These busy lives, whose brave sparks fly away,
One marble slab of fact alone survives.
Some write their virtues large with firm bold pen,
Others their frailties blot in tears of ink ;
Others, still climbing height on height in vain,
Leave sighs—breaks—blanks, right on—up to the
brink.

Some in invisible lines trace small and faint
That none may read life-secrets dead years wrote,
But the fire tests each record—sinner, saint,
Or dubious veiled guest last in Charon's boat.
Oh, for this epitaph when underground—
He left on earth more sunshine than he found !

ON A BELOVED ONLY SISTER.

I.

THY work is done, right nobly done, blest Soul !
  The energy of love, the toil, the pain,
  The thronging sympathies that knew no rein—
Life's grand unconscious pattern as a whole
Finished how suddenly ! abrupt the goal !
  That brimming heart of love, that busy brain,
  The will, the look, are ours no more again
For kindling converse, counsel, joy, control !

Thy will, O God, Thy mighty will be done !—
  Hers were such stores of life, such stores of love,
And our three souls were knit, so knit in one,
  I never dreamed Heaven could have needs above !
Forgive me, Father,—let all mine be Thine !
But know, O Father, this, all Thine is mine.

II.

I wept to think of her in her bright dress
   Of immortality and glory wove
By hands unfallen, hearts all sinlessness,
   That never knew the ache of human love !
And as the thoughts within me burned and strove,
   Her beauty but embittered my distress ;
And barren as some windswept nestless grove
   Seemed that fair land of everlastingness !

I longed to see her human as she was,
   Yearned for the working dress she used to wear—
The morning kiss that broke love's fast—the pause
   In daily toil so infinitely fair.
Yes, I shall see her, but transfigured !
Our human Annie is for ever dead.

III.

My sister, I am travelling, travelling now,
  To meet thee in that dreamland of pure love,
Where, like yon sun emerged from mountain's brow
  The cloudless soul soars luminous above—
Thou hast brought heaven so near, so very near,
  I seem to tread it even now with thee !
Life's mystery long dark, now startling clear,
  Runs on unbroken to eternity !

We both, enamoured of one Wounded Face
  That haunts both worlds alike, have by His will
At either side of Him a wondrous place,
  Thou in the sunshine, I in shadow still !
My sister, I will go down every day
To death's dim pier, till I too launch away !

IV.

But ah, loved brother, then hadst thou forgot
　　The glorious life-charge our great Master gave,
Sealed with the seal of Him who changeth not,
　　Into thy solemn keeping till the grave !
Wouldst seek death ?　Nay, seek life, long life o'erbrimmed
　　With living waters sparkling in the sun
Of righteousness !　Be vigilant, strong-limbed,
　　Heaven's mighty harvester ! thus glory's won.

With eyes dawn-fixed and trembling lips, go bear
　　The deathless secrets of eternity
To shadow-haunted souls, that cannot hear
　　Love's thronging tune creation's set to !　Cry—
Woo, strive not, live !　Live life with windows wide,
That all may see one mystic Form inside !

THE POOR ORGAN-GRINDER AT THE FUNERAL.

THE thronging nave was hushed—-a snowy pile
   Of victor wreaths and blossoms veiled the dead,
   And the whole sanctuary was perfumèd
With bloomy incense, lit with spring's fresh smile.
There 'mid the throng I spied far down the aisle
   A poor man's face deep hunger-worn, but fed
   With noble instincts unfulfilled indeed,
Till he too shall have trod death's dark defile.

She whom he mourned had rescued him long years
   From the fell tyranny of dire disease—
Dowered him with manhood, once a thing of tears;
   Hers his worn lute, still battling with the breeze.
Behold the epitaph God stoops to read—
Want's stricken face Love's glowing hands have freed!

THE SAINT'S ASCENSION.

HUDDLESTONE STOKES, ESQ.

Thou long hast been immortal, deathless Friend,
But now the veil is fallen, and we see
Thy white-robed soul triumphantly ascend,
Not dust to dust, but light to light for thee !
This law is for immortals—and the clay
Now riven in haste, bright angel feet of faith,
Casting their dusty sandals by the way,
Strike instant dawn out of the dark of death.

Never was nobler, truer, humbler soul
Borne into heaven by singing multitudes ;
And none e'er caught Christ's image grandly whole
In lowlier depths where penitence long broods.
No marvel thou didst pass without a sigh ;
Who dies each day he lives has nought to die !

ROBERT BROWNING.

Strong rugged world-seer! Though I knew thee not
   Whilst still on earth unburdening thy great soul
   Of mighty harmonies, that past control
Drove their fierce furrows of volcanic thought
Down culture's calm cheek—farewell! Thou hast
      fought
   Nobly. Fame breathless stood to watch thee bowl
   Thy flaming orb of song right home—the goal
Burned like the dawn though long the tempest
      wrought.

All minds and moods interpreting to men,
   Thou didst thyself all life impersonate ;
But ah, keen soul explorer, on thy ken
   Vast tracts of untrod Deity now wait !
Thine was no soft lute's murmuring rhythmic wind,
But thunder-throes of loosening blocks of mind !

GORDON.

One figure stands on the horizon's rim,
  Fair with an immortality unique
  In human story—great with deeds that speak
World-wide the imperishable fame of Him,
Who, though He dwell with burning seraphim,
  Dowers with His own omnipotence the meek—
  Heaven-hid till storms lower, like some iron peak
Etherealized by summer haze to dream.

Gordon, thou lost ideal of our time,
  Whilst men believe not, and belief grows pale
  Before the daring doubters that assail,
We need thy childlike faith, thy gaze sublime,
  That, piercing the near gloom, still onward strode
  Through death and darkness, seeing only God !

LORD MOUNT TEMPLE.

The world is colder since thy sun went down—
    Went down in splendour noiseless as thy life,
    Thou noble-hearted banisher of strife,
Thou tender traveller betwixt Cross and crown.
Heaven's own simplicity was thine—a light,
    The light of early dawn instinct with dews,
    Healing all sundered souls, thou didst diffuse,
Like summer twilight linking day and night.

Thy name was fraught with human brotherhood,
    Thy words down dropping softly everywhere
Like snowflakes fell, but straight unveiled there stood
    Truth's dauntless snow-peaks towering crystal fair;
Thy life soul-luminous, transparent, just,
Seemed God's own signature in human dust.

THE MARCHIONESS OF AILSA.

HIGH dews of grace lay on thee, Christ-like soul,
    Thou who serenely trod'st life's loftiest way.
    Veiled in the light of Heaven's unrisen day,
Lit with meek lustre from faith's unseen goal!
The sacred fire upon thine altar-heart,
    Kindled in secret by God's awful touch,
    Burned bright and brighter, till (God's favour such!)
All self-consumed, Love's flame too must depart!

Gentlest of living souls—ah! not in vain
    Those spotless years of tender stateliness
And unshed bloom thou liv'dst—though life's ripe
        grain
    Too soon Heaven garners—long shall brave souls
        press
Where thy frail vessel's wake, white without stain,
    Still lights dark seas with lasting loveliness!

SORROW'S BIRTHRIGHT.

Framed in white sorrow, that fair widowed face
   Breathes resignation forth from morn till eve
   Touched with soul-rapture, such as angels leave
In their swift wonder-wake's last dying trace.
Her love-tide's at the full, and pants for dawn,
   Unchanged, unchangeable, serener now !—
   Though storms have passed, and stripped the forest-
      bough
Bare of rich summer, blue heaven's closer drawn.

Wrecked 'mid the wrecked ? Nay, see one brave
      hand more
   Homeless outstretched where homeless ones abound,
Those wounds of hers best lure the wrecked to shore,
   Those dews of death best fructify the ground ;—
Those grand eyes, flashing beauty from their birth,
Shine Heaven-wed now—God's beacon-lights on
      earth !

THE EARL OF IDDESLEIGH.

A CHIEF has fallen, fallen gloriously—
    From stair to stair he climbed life's proudest stage,
    The dust of the arena his sole wage,
Save conscience shed a light that may not die.
Heaven was each day's near background, and his eye
    Caught gleams of peace from off Truth's charmèd
        page
    'Mid strife of empires,—and 'mid faction's rage
His life's horizon still touched quiet sky.
If behind foeman's steel he marked a friend,
    'Twas but to spare him nobly in the fight ;
Though principle to friendship durst not bend,
    High courtesy is honour's native light—
Duty's heaven's altar-stair—see, bright ascend
    Those brave steps—ah ! pathetically bright.

THE MIGHTY PAST.

Hail, spoils of past Humanity—rich sum
    Of Time's proud billows beating on the shore
    Of frail mortality for evermore !
Hail, wrecks of empires, from whose martyrdom
Rise victor voices regnant o'er the tomb,
    Unquenched, unquenchable, whose high souls soar—
    A nearer heaven for mankind to adore—
Still sovereign over ages yet to come !
A nation's soul's immortal, sphered sublime
    Above decay, like banner proud unfurled
With glorious legend and far-echoing chime,
    It heralds the world's dawn, night 'neath it hurled.
Humanity's the keyboard where in Time
    God plays rich preludes of some deathless world !

BY THE GRAVE OF CANON BATTERSBY
AT KESWICK.

Yet there's no change in Nature ! as of yore
The mighty hills couch grandly in the glow
Of evening's splendour ; yea, heaven's sunset gates
Westward, slow kindling into pomp, henceforth
Shall here for thee, who ever sought God's gate,
Break open daily at thy feet, O Friend,
Loved Friend, here laid in thy last resting-place,
Beside the trembling lake thou lov'dst so well,
With all its bays and purple promontories,
And wooded isles that float in liquid light,
Asleep on their own melting images
In conscious peace !

     But we, alas ! we mourn
That sacred Form withdrawn into the light—
Our loved one vanished from his own fair lake—
Who year by year was wont to welcome us
In golden summer-time beneath his roof,
With such meek chastened gaiety of soul

As more than aught about him else betrayed
His bosom's living Inmate—Ah, we mourn
That fair home's high simplicity—the step,
The light elastic step heard now no more—
The firm will sheathed in gentlest courtesy—
That high pale brow, that spiritual light
That dwelt there like the perfume in the flower
Unbound, yet by no wind of circumstance
Dislodged,—and all the halo of that life,
Which passing in and out cast everywhere
Its own white shadow unsuspectingly
To linger in the darkness, and to light
In other hearts the likeness of its own,
To God's high praise!   Ah, well did he engrave
His own fair epitaph abidingly
In other lives, which thus became his lips,
Now his, alas! lie silent in the dust,
To tell his Master's message unto men,
And wake the Christ within us.

                              Strange, indeed,
That last long week we spent in Conference
Between his death-bed and his open grave,—
That long week of strange twilight betwixt Time
And God's Eternity, when all seemed hushed

As some unearthly Presence unperceived
Had come and stood among us, and the door
Of the Unseen stood open at our side
And none dared shut it !

                    Strange to us indeed,
That he should lie by his loved Conference
All that long week of silence and speak not,
And yet no voice was sounding in all ears
Like *his*—the absent leader, teacher, friend,
Father, and counsellor, presiding still
With that persuasive, calm, and silvery smile
Of saintliest silence, like some lone high tarn
Trod by the riven cloud's tall slanting rays
In mystic stillness,—till The Tent's frail walls,
As by some sudden tide of glory pierced
And lost in the unutterable glow,
Dissolved before Faith's vision noiselessly,
And mortal with immortal in one band,
Like one unbroken family of light,
In awful fellowship seemed blended now
Before the immediate presence of The Throne—
There where the unveiled vision of High God
Mingling with earth's dim outer court again
Made Heaven and earth one, one for evermore !

Thus he in meekness proved himself to be,
Throughout long years of lowly ministry—
(Bear witness, ye ungrudging Brotherhood
Of kindred souls linked round his open grave!)
One of God's mountain messengers of light,
Whose feet stand on the mountains next the dawn;
And who from misty valleys upward lure
The fearful flock, and tempt to breezy heights
And thymy pastures sweetened by the sun!
Thus nobly didst thou set thyself, high Soul,
From doubt's cold chilling tenure to reclaim
Truth's waste crown-lands, reclaim them for the
    King,—
Thyself unworthy to thyself, but all
The consecration of the kingdom thine,—
Thou meek apostle of God's highest Truth,
Unrecognised defender of the Faith,
Who scorning ease, preferment, and high place,
All reputation to thy God resigned,—
Wearied with wrangling schools that, still unfed,
Unwearied wrangle o'er the Bread of Life,—
Thyself alone struck up the steep ascent
And white peaks of far holiness untrod,
And followed where Christ led, Heaven's light thy
    law!

ON THE DEATH OF AN INDEPENDENT STATESMAN.

WITH face of flint and eye of flame,
And cheeks that burned with noble shame,
He dared to call things by their name,
  And be unpopular !

But so his fame uprose to heaven,
By adverse winds of earth updriven,
Till guardian angels might have striven
  To tend those scouted steps.

From dark eyes hid 'mid rugged eaves,
Like windows opening on the leaves,
He poured such godlike soul as weaves
  A nation in its spell.

His high soul knew no ebbing tide,
But struggling factions stood aside,
As he strode forth with free-born stride
  To launch the law of Right.

He asked no favour, felt no fear,
Nor worshipped gold, nor courted peer,
Intent to catch his country's ear,
		And lead her back to light.

Erect he stood, heaven-taught, to teach,
No fingering of light coins of speech,
He bowed to none, so durst beseech
		His country for her weal.

Brave face soul-lit ! no eye could scan
That lofty brow, but feared its ban,
Nature had made him first a man,
		And then a nation's seer !

Thus stood he heart and conscience higher
Than genius kindling self's low fire,
His kingly spirit dared aspire
		To light the lamps of Truth !

HENRY F. BOWKER, ESQ.

Friend, teacher, leader, O beloved, revered !
   Veteran in arms, hast thou too conquered death ?
   Companion in a hundred fights of faith,   ·
Last of the Romans, who must needs be feared
Since greatly loved—Rest now ! High hadst thou
      reared
   And borne aloft until thy latest breath
   The standard of the Cross !—" He saved—He
      saith "—
These thy life's watchwords, henceforth death-en-
      deared.

Then, for the gradual breaking of the dawn,
   The gentle loosening of the pilgrim tent,
      For all that noble weight of mellowing years
      So lightly borne—Thank God ! And though our
            tears
   Blind the all-bright horizon, yet still bent
Upwards, we mount, till we too are withdrawn.

THE MARTYR MAIDEN.

   " I AM ready to die for the grace of God!
     He has brimmed my soul with His blameless bliss
   I could dare the stake with its surging crowd,
     And venomous taunts and the faggot's hiss.

   " I am ready to die for the grace of God!
     He has writ in deathless light on my soul;
   Such writing is quenched by no blood-stained sod,
     No hands can rend that immortal scroll.

   " I am ready to die for the grace of God!
     He has called me to join the immortal choir,
   And I care not how I reach His abode,
     By the light of love or the lamp of fire!

   " I am ready to die for the grace of God!"
     'Twas a dying girl in her orphaned home,
   And she longed to launch on the stormy flood,
     And each wail of the blast seemed the angels'
       " Come!"

" I am ready to die for the grace of God !"
  And her soul burnt through the transparent skin,
Like an altar-flame still athirst for food—
  'Twas God Himself had arrived within.

" I am ready to die for the grace of God !"
  And her dying hand fell pulseless, chill—
But the angels caught their triumphant load
  With a spirit shout !—But on earth, how still !

A CHILD'S EPITAPH.

WHEN from the ark the timid dove
  Stepped softly forth with beaming eye,
The patriarch watched in longing love
  Until it melted in the sky—
And it returned no more ; ah, sweet no more !
For then he knew that it had gained the shore—
So my wee dove stole softly from my breast,
And comes no more—she too hath found her rest !

THE WILDERNESS, WESTON UNDERWOOD, MAY-DAY.

Cowper, I've trod thy classic haunts to-day,
   And mused in silence through each shy retreat,
   Listening in vain to catch thine echoing feet
Still wandering pensive down life's chequered way.
Green earth was in her springtime—children gay
   With flowers and songs and streamers boisterous
     greet
   Each cottage door along the rustic street,—
Thy spirit lingers, though thou couldst not stay.
High in the elm-tree tops the wind-rocked rooks
   Sway in their noisy nests, as erst of old,
The woods are primrose-paved, and violet nooks
   O'errun with celandine's rich spendthrift gold—
And singing larks go up in sunlit bands
To waft love-tidings to Life's upper lands !

TO VISCOUNT EVERSLEY, ON HIS NINETY THIRD BIRTHDAY.

FOR MANY YEARS SPEAKER TO THE HOUSE OF COMMONS.

WELL-NIGH a century of years has rolled
   Eventful o'er thee, noble Eversley,
   Yet green and stately, stately as a tree
Built by slow time in some immortal mould,
Thou still abidest !—still by unseen hold
   Of central root shot down invisibly,
   Thou brav'st all shock of storms blown off the sea
Of Time unbent, magnificently bold !

Throughout long years of lofty rectitude
   Thy patriot soul steered onward without swerve
   'Mid surging senates, and with steadfast nerve
Held high the scales of honour, and still stood
Anchored to the unseen ; so didst thou serve
   God and thy conscience first, then all men's good.

Elliot Stock, Paternoster Row, London.